Bottling His Ghosts

S.H. Cooper

Bottling His Ghosts © 2025 by S.H. Cooper

Published by Raw Dog Screaming Press
Bowie, MD

First Edition

Cover art copyright 2025 by Lynne Hansen
LynneHansenArt.com
Book design by Stephanie Pearre

Printed in the United States of America

ISBN: 978-1-947879-92-8
Library of Congress Control Number: 2025937030

RawDogScreaming.com

Other Books by S.H. Cooper

The Corpse Garden

From Twisted Roots

All That's Fair

Inheriting Her Ghosts

The Ungodly Duology

Threads of Ash: South

Reap, Sow

Acknowledgements

Bottling His Ghosts had an interesting development compared to my other books. I'll be the first to admit I'm a fairly slow writer, preferring to follow wherever my fancy leads to whatever story it so desires. I'd had the rough idea for this book floating around in my head since finishing its spiritual predecessor, *Inheriting Her Ghosts*, two years earlier in 2021. It was little more than a couple of plot points and the silhouette of a main character when I saw Raw Dog Screaming Press announce they were opening submissions for novellas. I'd seen many calls like it, imagined how nice it would be to have something to send in, and usually carried on my merry way. This time, however, was…different. I did have something – an idea, anyway – and three weeks to write it.

In those three weeks, champion of indie writers everywhere and incredible author in her own write (pun fully intended), **Laurel Hightower** acted as sounding board, confidence booster, and cheerleader. She provided boundless enthusiasm for my ideas and helped me fight off imposter syndrome whenever it reared its ugly head. I am forever grateful to call her my friend.

Burrowed in the trenches beside me while I wrote my heart out was **ESB**. There's no one made of sterner stuff and when I doubted myself, they were always there to (lovingly) kick my butt and get me back on track. There are few people I trust to be as honest and genuine in their feedback and friendship. Everyone should be so lucky to have an ESB in their life.

I would like to thank **R.J. Joseph** for seeing something special in this story and selecting it to be part of her novella lineup. This is one of my most personal, cherished tales to date and I'm incredibly thankful she has given me the chance to share it.

Finally, I am so thrilled I got to work with **Raw Dog Screaming** Press to make BHG a reality. A big thank you to **Jennifer Barnes** for being so great to work with and making this such a wonderful experience.

For the SHC who came before me, who held my hands once so I would walk, and again so I would dance.

For Ma and Dad, who have always encouraged me to spread my wings and are ever ready with a soft place to land.

For Alex, 'til you're 70 (at the very least).

Chapter One

I have a story that is not mine to tell.

Not in whole, anyway, for I am but a peripheral character who fancied herself part of the main cast. Is that not the hubris of us all, believing ourselves to hold a more central place on the world's stage than our billing truly allows?

But, if not for that very hubris, I would have had no role at all.

I know he would have preferred it that way.

But that comes later, I suppose, for this is the beginning, and it began, as many things do, in anger.

I had much to be angry about. A widow at five and twenty after only two years spent with my beloved. They called it an unfortunate mishap. An act of God. Whatever terms are assigned to make a steel mill accident more palatable to the grieving wife. They, the foremen and my father-in-law, would not provide exact details, fearing they were too gruesome for the delicate state of a woman cloaked in new mourning. I am yet undecided as to whether or not I am grateful for their sensitivity. I doubt I will ever truly know my husband's final moments, or whether I really want to.

Regardless, Victor was gone, and I was left to occupy the space we'd made for both of us, surrounded by his absence even as friends and family attempted to fill it. In the days following his funeral, they orbited as a herd, bringing me food, attempting consolation through their company.

Truthfully, I resented them for it. For not being my husband, the only person who had any hope of easing the yoke upon my heart.

Then, slowly, they broke away, a trickle that turned to a flood until I alone remained in the wretched aftermath.

I hated them for that too.

That was how I spent my waking hours, at violent odds with a world that I no longer knew my place in. There had been plans, a lifetime of them. The wedding, which I got, and children, which I did not. There should have been years more of rushed mornings where just a single, last minute kiss turned to three or four until I had to push him out the door with laughter and his taste upon my lips. There should have been years more of fireside evenings, where the dark outside our window could not touch us. There should have been years more of life, with all its fervour and fury and the bittersweet heartache born from souls entwining so completely.

Instead, I was left with only the bitter. Only the ache.

The city we had made ours was tarnished, a promise left unfulfilled. The friends I had made were strangers now, knowing only Mrs. Victor Ward and never Netta. I became a lonely, loathsome creature, haunting the remnants of us that Victor left behind.

I'm sure the insurance policy Victor had obtained without my knowledge was meant to be his final comfort, but it served a stinging blow, reducing the worth of my husband to a monetary amount that could never match the value of the man himself.

Every coin earned from that policy came tinted in red visible only to me.

I was only too happy to see it spent on the train tickets north, to home.

I wrote ahead without detail beyond my expected arrival and filled a single trunk with as much as it would hold. I did not think about what would happen to our small terrace house or the things inside it. I did not think about my employ under Mrs. Mayberry or who would take my position in the millinery shop.

I thought only of the train, and the many miles that would soon separate me from all the empty tomorrows.

I had hours to think in that train car, for mine was not the mood for pleasantries or taking part in the conversations of my seatmates. They, a pair of women so close in resemblance looking at the mother was a glimpse into the daughter's future, made a polite attempt to invite my input, but I could only contrive the palest of smiles and adjust my veil to better shield myself from them. The daughter clucked her tongue in reproof, but her mother shifted nearer to her and, in a quiet utterance not meant for me to hear, begged her patience on account of my mourning gown.

Standing upon the station platform in my black bombazine and crape had roused similar hushed reactions, from the pitying to the speculative, more concerned with whether I had properly observed my required period of isolation than the event that made it necessary to begin with.

Yes, I wanted to cry, *I am left a widow! Made to wear my loss like a banner, signalling my grief for all to see.*

How I would have liked to claw that black from my body and flee faster and farther than the train allowed, as if removing the public symbol of my status would somehow strip the pain as well.

My hands wound together in my lap, twisting with them the wedding band concealed 'round my finger by my glove. I did not need to feel it in detail to know its every inch, the delicate feather motif decorating its rose gold band, the circle of tiny diamonds surrounding its emerald centre.

None of those jewels would ever shine so bright as did my Victor's eyes, green as the stone he'd placed upon my finger with his promises of everlasting love.

11

And love everlasting I still had, for with Victor went my heart, then and always, though I felt none of God's grace in it anymore. Only a hollow cold no fire could ever quench.

Overcome, I muffled my sobs into a hastily produced handkerchief while the pair across from me had the courtesy to avert their gazes.

I made my escape from the confines of the train car as soon as I was permitted to do so, eager to put my travel and the embarrassment of my fragile emotions behind me. Upon being reunited with my trunk, delivered by a courteous porter who left it against a wall to avoid cluttering the walkway, I searched the crowd for my father, the one most likely tasked with fetching me. Though average in height and soft around the belly, particularly in the most recent years, his was a distinctive gait, straight-backed with a bull's authority. I would have noticed his approach carving a path through the bedlam of disembarking passengers immediately.

But the swirl of strangers remained uncut, and I unclaimed.

As the platform began to empty with no sign of Father, I was left to ponder his uncharacteristic delay, and the mundane excuses piled quickly into darker suggestions. Though not a terribly long carriage ride, there were desolate points between the farm and the station, and at any one, he might suffer some hardship. A small misstep might lame a horse or snap a wheel, leaving him stranded.

The cape buttons clasped at my throat took the brunt of my worry, twisted between restless fingers while I watched the entrance.

"Henrietta?"

The sound of my name spoken from behind while all my attention was focused so keenly ahead sent my heart skipping. I turned, lips parted in a gasp that rose from alarm into relief.

"Mr. Bentley!"

His moustache, thick as a caterpillar across his upper lip and almost as lively, turned up in a warm smile that I was able to return with full sincerity. My family's longtime solicitor, and my father's dear friend for even longer, I'd always regarded Crawford Bentley with the fondness of a niece for her uncle, but I had never been happier to see him than in that moment.

"Did you accompany Father?" I queried, looking past him. "Or did you come in his stead? It's not that I'm not pleased to see you, of course, only that I expected–" The befuddlement spreading behind his spectacles halted my speech. "Father did send you, didn't he?"

"I'm sorry, I don't know what you mean, my dear. I've only just returned from a lecture down south on this same train." At the slow sinking of my shoulders, he leaned in with concerned paternal airs. "Were you expected?"

"I should have been. I sent a telegram last week."

"I informed him of my travel dates, but he failed to mention our shared arrival. If he had known, I'm sure I would've heard of it. There must have been some mistake at the post office and I fear word never reached your family." Mr. Bentley exhaled brusquely and offered his arm with renewed good humour. "What luck we happened upon each other then, hmm? I have a carriage waiting already. Don't fret, we will get you home."

I did attempt to entertain Mr. Bentley's running commentary, ranging from his unfavourable opinions of congested city life to the enthusiastic observation of grazing livestock, but could hardly muster more than the occasional nondescript sound in reply, which did little to discourage him. On the contrary, he filled in my silences himself and was entirely content to provide both questions and answers.

For all his rambling, kept noticeably to lighter subjects, never once did he broach the topic of my late husband or catch his tongue on awkward commiserations, something that did not go unappreciated.

Being allowed to forgo the burden of managing someone else's sympathy was, while selfish, very welcome.

We rounded the sloping curve of my family's drive as afternoon waned into evening. The weak September sun sat atop the roof's peak, dusting the brown stone front in pale gold. Once a modest farmstead, four generations of Father's family had built up and expanded upon their forebearer's success, leaving Daunderhead Hall and all its surrounding acres as their legacy.

Crisp, sweet air, free of the city's smoke and smells, enveloped me as I stepped from the carriage, assisted by the driver's steadying hand. While he retrieved my trunk, I gazed upon my girlhood home, at the creeping vines that bloomed green and purple around the windows, up to the chimney stacks and their curls of smoke, to the carthouse and the lane beyond, leading to the farmhand cottages. Exactly as it had always been.

Its unchanging nature, which had never failed to evoke such tranquillity in me before, struck me suddenly as vulgar mockery, ignoring the world outside its walls to continue on in ignorant bliss as if never touched by life's cruel shadows. How could it remain so when I had been forced to swallow so much sorrow and been altered so irrevocably? How could I ever know that same sense of peace again now that I recognized it for the falsehood it truly was?

I wanted to rage against Daunderhead and beat upon its stones for not crumbling with me.

Tears blurred it all into a wash of indistinct colour and I again withdrew my handkerchief to dab its black borders against my eyes before Mr. Bentley came around the carriage to escort me to the door.

It was opened promptly by a willowy maid in uniform who dropped into a curtsy upon recognizing her guests.

"Miss Henrietta," she said, blue eyes wide as milk saucers. "Mr. Bentley."

"Hello, Florence," I tried to summon some expression of warmth, but my features hung grim and listless. "Are my parents in?"

"Yes, ma'am. Please." She stepped aside, pulling the door wider with her as a gesture for us to enter. "May I take your cape?"

"If you would." I shed the outer garment and handed it off, but Mr. Bentley declined with a wave of his fingers.

"I won't be staying, thank you. Please, let Mrs. Alden know Mrs. Ward has arrived."

Florence dipped shallowly again and scurried from the foyer down the west hall, toward the drawing room where Mother often spent her after supper hours.

Mr. Bentley turned to me, tender affection worn plainly, and in it, I could read the impending mention of my husband. Displeasure curled my toes within my carriage boots.

"I'm sorry about Victor, Henrietta. If there's anything I can do, please do not hesitate to reach out. My firm is at your disposal."

"Thank you."

My unwillingness to extend my gratitude any further left little room for either of us to say more. Being an estate solicitor, Mr. Bentley was well acquainted with all manner of disposition that followed the death of a loved one, and nothing in his farewell, wherein he bid me to pass on his greeting to my parents, indicated any insult. He tipped his tall hat and withdrew, pulling the door closed behind him.

I stood so small in that entryway, the same that had welcomed me all my life. Each painting upon the wall, every bust, vase, and crease in the burgundy wallpaper was as familiar to me as my own skin. The aroma of the recent meal could have been drawn straight from any of my countless memories. I could traverse the immediate grounds with my eyes closed, never stumbling or losing my place.

It was home.

It should have been home.

But there was none of Victor in it, and the repeated offence of Daunderhead's indifference overwhelmed me to such degree that I nearly screamed.

A flurry of footsteps sounded in the west hall, and Mother burst into the foyer, the train of her dark tea dress dragging carelessly behind her. Gentle confusion furrowed her brow. "Netta? What are you doing here? Is everything alright?"

It only took the sight of her to extinguish my impotent fury. No more was I a wife or widow railing against an unjust fate. The loneliness and despair that had hounded me since the steel mill representative appeared on my doorstep, cap crumpled in his fists and head bowed, erupted like a boil upon my soul. Before her, with my trembling hands outstretched, I became a needful child again, adrift in an anguish that staggered me.

And as I began to fall, succumbing at last to my tormented heart, it was into her arms and against her breast, and she held me tight while I shattered.

Chapter Two

What followed was only fragments. Father called from his office or billiard room, my face cupped in his earnest grasp, so many questions, then I was being supported up the stairs, into a room, and Mother and Florence were moving around me, stripping me of my gown and loosening my stays. They positioned me as if I were a doll, gently turning me this way and that while Mother bathed my limbs with a sponge soaked in warm water and Florence unpinned my hair.

I observed their actions through a dream-like lens, neither helpful nor combative, hardly there at all except in body. Existence had become too heavy a burden and my senses had flown, leaving only a keening ring to fill my head.

The next I was aware, I was tucked into bed with Mother stroking my cheek, imploring me to sleep.

A baby's cry carried distantly through the darkness.

I fought against its rousing qualities, threatening to return me to consciousness, but it persisted into a wail that I could not ignore.

In my sleep soaked mind, I initially believed it to be the product of a dream I'd yet to fully shake. It would not have been the first time I dreamt of the children denied to me, their plaintive cries taunting me while I tore through rooms both known to me and strange in search of them. I'd wake to a pillow damp with tears and a womb that ached with its emptiness.

This time, however, opening my eyes did not dispel the faint weeping.

I'd slept through whatever daylight had been left and sat up to a room pitched in black, though the dark held no secrets for me. I knew immediately the shape of the vanity, the writing table, the armoire angled in the corner. My room, arranged still to my liking as it had been on my wedding day, the last I had lived in it.

The only change came from that sound, not heard within Daunder-head's walls for decades.

An infant.

I threw back my blankets and crawled to the edge of my bed, listening. When still the thin peal wafted through the house, I fell back on my heels, grasping the bodice of the nightgown Mother had changed me into. My heart pattered beneath the cotton, spurred by an unease that sank into my belly and spread with the chill of a winter's fog.

I set one foot upon the floor, breath held to better hear the babe, followed by the other, and rose with quivering slowness. On the child wept, softer now, as if moving away from me across the ground floor. I urged it to fade completely, to prove itself a phantom constructed from my longing, but was granted no such reprieve.

I thought not to follow it, that I might bury myself once more beneath my covers and drown out its cries with my own, certain that entertaining such a manifestation would only serve to open myself up to more hurt. In effort to banish it, I clapped my hands over my ears and it did quell the sound, but in the ensuing, miserable silence, a second notion began to take hold, as irrational and desperate as I'd ever allowed myself: That it was Victor somehow come back to me, carrying with him our future, and they were looking for me.

It did not matter that it defied every ounce of reason I possessed, for love and loss ask not for fact, only faith, and my wounded spirit yearned so much for my husband that I could believe my desire alone was enough to recall him to my side.

What other explanation could there be, especially on the eve of my return?

So taken with this fantasy, I clamoured to my three panel privacy screen and reached for the dressing gown I'd always hung there, only for my fingertips to meet painted wood instead. In my urgency, I had reverted to habits that would of course be outdated since my going. I again clutched the collar of my nightgown. To leave the room in only my bed clothes would be unseemly, particularly if I came across Father. I could not! But neither could I stay. I circled in place, hoping to locate my trunk, but it had not been brought up yet, leaving me with no alternative to my present state of undress.

Finally, unable to withstand the now nearly imperceptible mewls and all that they could represent any longer, I swept the decorative quilt top from my bed and wrapped it around my shoulders as a makeshift shawl before hurrying from my room.

The hall was long and dark, made more precarious by my wobbling legs, turned nearly to gelatin by the discord raging within me. With one step, I would tell myself it could not be Victor, and most certainly not our offspring who had never existed, only for my next step to fall on impossible hope, that he had not died at all and the last three months had been the dream and this, being woken so while only visiting my parents, was real.

The life I was meant to be leading.

I made it to the top of the stairs and leaned heavily upon the bannister. A flickering strip of light stretched across the floor below, cast from the partially open parlour, and with it came not the cry, but a murmur. A man's voice, though kept so low it was impossible to determine anything else about it. Still, my heart leapt. Surely, surely it had to be him! By God's good will, he'd been returned to me! I stifled a weak inhale in my knuckles and lunged without grace, hand over hand upon the railing, down the staircase, and across the foyer to throw wide the doors with a jubilant declaration.

"Victor!"

But it was Father who whirled 'round, startled both my entrance and the near miss of the doors swinging open at his back. As our eyes met, the sorry illusion I'd conjured fractured and fell to pieces, as did my heart all over again, and the final vestiges of denial I hadn't realised I was clinging so tightly to slipped, at last, away.

Had I really expected to find my departed husband standing before the crackling hearth when I flung open the parlour? In the few euphoric, foolish breaths where hope had found a way to grow, perhaps. Now faced undeniably with the reality of my situation, it could only ever have been delusion. I was no wife, never a mother, only a silly, sad girl in her nightclothes and a quilt.

The reminder of my indecent dress made me hug the quilt closer against me and I averted my gaze, heavy with embarrassment and fresh sorrow, to the floor.

"Father," I said, unsure how to even begin to explain myself.

"Is that Netta?"

That Father was in his dressing gown, an abnormality outside of his room save for times of illness, should have told me right away that something was amiss, but I'd hardly registered it. The fact he wasn't alone had escaped me entirely. So when someone spoke from behind him, I jumped, surprised, and peered sharply over his shoulder.

A woman of my similar age was seated on the sofa beside Mother, likewise in her nightdress. Bundled in her arms was a baby, asleep now, though reddened cheeks proved hers had been the cries that had woken me. The sight of her came as a ray of sunlight through the shaded veil of my bereavement and I nearly wept again from the rush of joy.

"Birdie!" I stepped forward, modesty momentarily forgotten as I went to embrace her.

She untucked one of her arms from beneath the child, Tabitha, to return it with equal fervour. Though we lived in the same city, it was at opposite ends, and our opportunities to visit one another had been limited, especially following Victor's tragedy. Unable to make or receive social calls during the early days of my full mourning, I had not spoken to her since before Tabitha's birth. Seeing the little one now, so soon after my latest upset, created such a conflict of emotion in me that I could not bring myself to pay the customary compliments. I instead focused on Birdie herself. "What are you doing here?"

"I could ask the same of you," she said.

"Where's Thorn?"

At the mention of her husband's name, Birdie's expression pickled into a sour line and she adjusted the swaddling around her daughter. Mother shifted uncomfortably beside her and I looked between them, concern tainting the delight their presence had brought me.

"Is everything alright?"

"We hadn't wanted to trouble you with any of this," Mother said reservedly. "You were already under such horrible strain."

I sat tepidly on the other side of Birdie with a frown. "Any of what?"

"Your cousin is unwell," she began, cut short by Father's malcontent scoff.

"Unwell? He's the source of all his own problems, Leonora."

"Edmund," Mother chastised him softly, sensitive to Birdie's apparent unhappiness, but he pressed on.

"I told your brother-in-law that saddling him with that name would come as a curse, but punishment was his priority. Well, look where it's got him now, the bloody sod!"

"Mind your language!"

After marriage to a labourer, I had grown accustomed, even comfortable, with most colourful turns of phrase, but even had that not been the case, my concern would not have been with my father's word choice.

21

Thorn's name had always been a source of vexation for my parents, that much did not surprise me. His mother had died upon the birthing bed and his father, made cruel by grief, had bestowed upon his newborn son a name that would never allow him to forget his supposed first deed. Forever would he be the thorn that robbed his mother of life.

Mother, sister to the deceased, had pleaded with him to reconsider, but my uncle refused. Moved by her compassion, Father then attempted to bribe him in return for a Christian name but again was turned away. Powerless to affect any change, the boy was so named, and, Father believed, the poor foundation of his life set.

And it was true that Thorn had been a troubled youth. Though born of good stock to a family in the banking industry, his had always been an impish disposition and mischief came naturally to him. What little thought his father paid to him, offering no discipline to right his wrongs, was lessened more after his remarriage, then eradicated completely upon the arrival of his subsequent children.

Thorn was only ten years old when he finally ran afoul of the law, caught picking pockets outside public houses. When no one from his paternal side moved to claim him, it was my parents who stepped forward, and thus I found myself quite unexpectedly with a brother four years my senior. His first year in our home, suddenly constricted with rules and responsibility, had been a tumultuous one, but both Mother and Father were determined to set him right. Being made to tend the sheep alongside their shepherds exhausted him beyond the point of mischief making and rigorous schooling, though never his strongest suit, occupied his mind enough to keep it off of less savoury pursuits.

Under their firm, but ever forgiving guidance, Thorn had bloomed into an upright and honourable man, eventually joining the very force he'd once pit himself against and rising to the rank of coroner's officer.

Or so I had thought.

"Has something happened to him?" I asked, cautious of my approach while my father's temper seemed so volatile.

Birdie's expression waned into removed indifference as she brushed a strand of golden hair from Tabitha's forehead. "He's taken to the bottle."

"It's pathetic," Father snapped, tightening the cord of his dressing gown. "Drowning himself when he has a family to consider."

"Children change things. Two months is hardly a long adjustment period," Mother said, ever a diplomat in matters relating to Thorn. The difficulties of his early life had left her with a tender spot that still sought to protect him from further hardship.

"Had this only been a habit since Tabitha was born, I might agree, but it began before then," Birdie replied with an acidic undertone.

I stopped the brewing squabble with a groaning touch to my temple, dizzy with only these bare slivers of information I could not piece together to create a whole story. I had stumbled into a conversation half-done and was expected to glean the point of it without knowing how it had started in the first place.

"Oh, darling," Mother fretted upon seeing my distress. "This is why we didn't tell you. You're in no position to be burdened further."

I waved her concern away with a shake of my head. "How did this happen? Last we wrote, he seemed in such good spirits."

Saying it aloud forced me to confront just how long ago that truly had been. Could our last correspondence really have been more than six months prior? I had been so consumed in my own misfortune I had not noticed the passage of time. Mother had kept me abreast of the goings on within the family, or the positive aspects of them anyway, as it now appeared, so it never felt like Thorn and I lost contact.

"It was gradual," Mother said.

"But why? Things were going well, weren't they, Birdie?"

She straightened, as if preparing to defend herself, though I didn't believe anything in my inquiry could be construed as an

23

attack. "They were, or so I thought. You know how Thorn is. How could I possibly know what's been going on inside his head?"

It was true that my cousin was a tight-lipped figure, rarely one for divulging his innermost machinations, but I had assumed his wife would be more in tune than I. Another misconception on my part.

"Where is he now?" I asked, looking around as if only becoming aware of his absence. "How did you come to be here?"

She sniffed, rocking Tabitha slightly in what seemed an excuse to keep from meeting my gaze. "When I left, he was still in the cottage. I couldn't stand it anymore, having to be around him like that. The walk was preferable to his company."

"The cottage?"

"They've been staying in one of the old shepherd's quarters for the last month," Father explained roughly. "Since Thorn was relieved of his position with the coroner's office. They couldn't risk a drunkard obstructing their cases."

I pushed myself off the sofa with an urgency that gave the others a start. "What condition was he in when you left?"

"Do not concern yourself," Father said.

"What condition!"

There had been many a lush in Victor's circle, common enough amongst working men, and I'd been regaled with more than one tale of maiming injury and untimely end due to the drink. The thought of my cousin left alone in a stupor, too in his cups to properly care for himself, was a terrible one I could not abide.

"As you would imagine," Birdie said with a scowl. For whom it was meant, my cousin or myself for prying, I did not know.

I spun from the room, letting my quilt fall away in my haste, and Father called after me. "Henrietta! Where are you going?"

"To find my trunk and dress," I said. "I must see Thorn."

Chapter Three

Father argued with me while I, without reaction, pulled clothing from my trunk, stored temporarily in the closet at the back of the stairs. Once I locked myself in the ante hall lavatory to dress, he turned his complaints on Mother. I listened to him through the door whilst I fastened my ribbon corset, carrying on about propriety, the late hour, the disruption to his sleep. Whatever Mother said in return was more subdued, too muffled to hear clearly, but it ebbed Father's bluster and he stomped up the steps with such a racket I knew it was meant for me.

I left my nightgown pooled on the floor and stepped into the day dress I'd selected at random. It was only as I began buttoning it that I took notice of its colour, green with small pink flowers, and my progress slowed. I had not worn anything but black since Victor's death and still had months left before it would be acceptable for me to adopt any variation. To adorn something brighter would be a betrayal of my station and greatly disrespect my husband's memory. Had Victor been able to, what might he have said on the matter?

His voice did come to me and with it reproach, but not for my attire. He wouldn't have cared at all what colour or pattern I adopted, especially not at such a critical time. He would have encouraged me, told me to wear whatever was at hand if it meant reaching Thorn sooner. And still, he would have found a moment to laugh at the improper fit of my dress, without undergarments to fill out its skirt.

I lifted my wedding ring to my lips and pressed upon it an ardent kiss, grateful to have felt his presence, however fleeting.

When I came from the lavatory, Mother was helping Father into a sack coat, having already swapped his nightclothes for those he'd been wearing when I arrived. He fixed me with an exasperated look and wagged a finger as if I were still a child to be scolded.

"This is folly," he said. "It's half a mile down the lane to the cottages, at least a ten minute walk, if not made longer by the dark."

"One Birdie made with a baby on her hip," I reminded him.

It did nothing to endear him to me.

"You do not need to come, Father. I know the way well enough on my own."

"Stop being ridiculous, both of you." Mother brushed her hands across Father's shoulders with more vigour than necessary before turning her narrowed gaze on me. After only a single look, she swept past to the coat rack, where my cape hung, having been taken from me at some earlier point.

"There's a chill," was all she said as she clasped my cape over my shoulders, donning me once more in widowhood. Stepping back to provide a final assessment, she nodded primly, then inhaled, a governess overseeing unruly pupils. "I shall stay with Birdie. Your father will accompany you to look in on Thorn and *you* will conduct yourself more accordingly. Our family has enough strife without hot heads prevailing. Who else do we have to rely on in times of duress if not each other? When one is in need, it is shared amongst us all. Now wait a moment and I will fetch a lantern from the kitchen to make your way easier."

Having successfully admonished us, she bustled down the hall, leaving us in subdued silence while we awaited her return.

Though I had often trod the laneways around Daunderhead, it had always been during the daytime. After dark, the paths lost their familiarity, changing to crooked snakes, and I shied from the heather borders with their purple blooms I so loved, suddenly wary of what lay beyond them. Father marched ahead without any such apprehension, making his displeasure known in exaggerated huffs.

His grumbling receded once we'd put the house behind us and for a time there was silence save for the breeze whispering across far off sheep fields. The half moon sat cradled in a gathering of clouds, its pale reach offering little to see by outside the light of our lantern. That Thorn occupied much of my attention, shifting between the brotherly figure with a ready smile that I was accustomed to and this yet unmet variant he had become, was a tiny blessing that soon distracted me from any skittish tendencies.

What awaited us ahead? The sombre moods of my family left me no reason to believe he'd be a jolly drunk. Initially, I'd been fearful for him, but could there be reason to be fearful *of* him? I'd witnessed a few altercations brought about by the bottle during evenings out with Victor and they had been messy affairs with no civil restraint. Birdie had not seemed frightened and showed no outward sign of abuse, but he might take differently to myself and Father. Thorn had never been a violent man, but never had he been a drinker either. At his size, an imposing height and muscled from years of farm work, it would not take much effort to deliver hard blows.

Try as I might, though, I simply could not reconcile such an idea of him with the version I knew in my heart.

In front of me, Father's gait had slowed to a ponderous pace, and I, without realising it, had followed suit, until we were only ambling along.

"Do you remember why it's called Daunderhead?" he asked unexpectedly, voice kept soft in volume and tone.

I furrowed my brow at such an out of place question, but answered, "Because of your great-grandfather, isn't it?"

"Correct, but beyond that; why he chose it?"

"No."

He sighed, a light, nostalgic sound I had not heard from him before. "Ours were not farming folk back then. When first we came, it was to a village smaller than the one you know now, where we had no stake and our name meant nothing. To set down roots here was the dream of an aimless man, who took no satisfaction from the life his family had offered, but had no vision of his own. Not until he laid claim to what was little more than a hovel and the hills around it, and he saw how he could grow. It was his restless mind that brought him here and gave birth to our line, and it was that same mind that was never content to settle. Daunderhead is a tribute to that quality he wished to sew in all of us; the freedom to deny stagnation and let your thoughts wander unfettered, always seeking more."

"Yes, I remember," I said. It was a story I'd heard before, mostly from my grandfather as a child, but years had passed since its last telling and the details had dulled with time. While it did muster fond memories of loved ones past, I could not fathom why Father had chosen to mention it now.

He'd tilted his head back slightly, toward the stars, and I hung at his back, curious over this contemplative air that had fallen over him. "I've begun to worry of late that I took its meaning too close to heart. While you and Thorn were in your most impressionable years, I was always looking for ways to improve business and provide more of everything but myself."

"What do you mean?"

"If I had been more available to both of you..." He trailed off, leaving his thought incomplete.

He'd said enough, however.

My engagement to Victor had been a sore subject. Mother and Father had envisioned a very different man for me, one who came from similar breeding. Any of the surrounding gentleman farmer's sons would have been far more ideal, allowing Father a son-in-law with whom he could have shared trade talk and, given that Thorn's interests diverted in adulthood, taken under his wing as a potential successor to his flock. I'd had every intention of following through with their plan – attending every party and ball to which I was invited with the mindset that I might meet my future husband there.

But God divined otherwise.

For it must have been through His intervention that Victor and I had our chance meeting within the Lord's own house. He'd been visiting with relatives in the village, a holiday that extended by days more after our first encounter and carried on in secret letters once he could no longer delay his return to the city. All along I'd known that my parents, particularly Father, would never approve of a craftsman's son, and it pit me terribly against myself. My duty as a daughter had always been of the utmost importance to me and I strived to perform in ways that would only make my family proud, but I could not deny that from the first I'd seen him, I was in love with Victor Ward.

Six months after our courtship began, Victor came back to the village, this time with a ring, and I knew there could be no more hiding.

Father and I never fought like we did that night I revealed my truth, voices raised and faces burned red with passion. Mother pleaded with me to reconsider and told me I was only taken by youthful fancy, not true love. We would return to the same quarrel many a time over the following days, never getting closer to a resolution. It was the only thing I'd ever stood my ground over so fiercely. Father demanded to know what had become of his child because the stubborn mule before him was certainly not his Henrietta. I would in turn shout that he could not be my father, for he always kept my happiness closest to his heart, unlike this selfish creature wearing his suit.

29

It was Victor who finally brought peace when he came to Daunderhead and requested an audience with my father.

They disappeared for hours into his study and I paced from drawing room to parlour, chewing my nails and disrupting my curls in worry. Unable to stand my fitful patrols, Mother went away to her chambers, leaving me to dwell in uncertainty on my own. When they emerged close to evening, it was under some solemn agreement between men that I was never fully privy to. However they came to it, Father granted his permission, and I soon wed my beloved. He never took to the idea of my employment or that I lived so far away from the countryside in such small quarters, but he was able to admit later that I had found my match and, though not ideal for him, my marriage befitted me.

So, when Victor passed in a workman's accident, Father took partial blame for my pain.

He thought if he'd made a different decision that day, unswayed by whatever Victor had said and my persistence, he could have saved me from my grief. It remained one of his deepest regrets.

For such a failure, at least he'd had Thorn.

What a small comfort that was as the lane widened and a row of closely nested cottages took the place of the heather. Most were shuttered, their thatched roofs in need of new straw and the doors swollen in their frames since Father had constructed newer lodging farther afield for the farmhands. There had been some plan for these, to either tear them down to expand the garden or build a second stable for the ponies. Mother could never decide what she truly wanted, but none had ever come to fruition.

One in the line stood apart, its windows left open to invite the night air. An orange glow, not strong enough to be the product of a hearth fire, emanated from inside, giving only the shallowest indication of life. Father and I paused as one before we reached the door, neither telling the other we had meant to do so. Apprehension gripped my chest and my teeth raked lightly along my lower lip.

"You may wait here," Father said. His demeanour had hardened again, losing all brooding qualities. "In fact, it might be preferable."

"No, I'll go."

"You've not seen your cousin in this way, Netta. It would be better if you didn't."

"I said I'll go."

I took point then, fingers curled into the front of my cape, and strode to the door. When my knocks went unheeded and Thorn did not answer to the sound of his name, Father waved me aside and grasped the knob. It wrested open with some coaxing and Father held the lantern aloft, better illuminating the gloom within.

Attempts at repair had been made to make the main room more livable. Some bricks had been replaced in the hearth and sheepskin rugs laid across the floor to better maintain warmth. Heavy drapes that Mother had sent to attic storage once they fell out of fashion were hung over one window, but another set was left folded on a chair with its rod laid across it. A sofa and armchair, more of Mother's storage pieces, were placed around the cold fireplace, overfilling the small main room and leaving space for little else, though a desk had been made to fit at an odd angle, paired unusually with a rocking chair that nearly blocked the narrow staircase leading upward.

It was empty of person and the light we'd seen through the window proved to come from the kitchen, situated at the back of the cottage.

"Thorn," Father called, giving him another chance to answer before we invited ourselves inside.

When the house remained silent, Father dragged a hand down his beard and exhaled through flaring nostrils before leading me through the tight passageway of furniture, to the kitchen.

First, I saw bottles. They crowded on the table around a single lit candle, most upright, though some were knocked askew, with drops hanging from open mouths and soaking into the rough hewn wood top. In the closet-sized scullery, dishes stacked high in the wash basin and spilled onto the counter with food still stuck to their surfaces. It was difficult to tell if it was all from supper or carried over from earlier meals. The window over it, along with the door at the rear, were open and the air that rolled in was damp and cold.

I crossed to close them, and that was when I saw him, slumped on the floor with a chair turned sideways beside him. Dark stubble covered his jaw in ungroomed patches and his hair had grown to shaggy lengths. He wore no jacket or waistcoat, only a white shirt stained in spots down its front, and the heady stench of ale was all around him. I gasped and dropped immediately to his side, brushing greasy strands from his face. I whispered a grateful prayer when I saw the rise and fall of his chest.

"Thorn? Can you hear me?"

"He can't," Father said. The lantern landed upon the table with a weighted thud that rattled the bottles.

"Should we send for the doctor?"

"No, he's not ill, only drunk."

"But he's not waking up!"

Father took me by the upper arm and lifted me once more to my feet. He then assumed my previous position, crouching over Thorn's prone form. "He won't for hours yet if this collection here is anything to go by."

His voice was level, dispassionate, and I wondered where the remorseful concern he'd shown on the way here had gone.

"What do we do?" I asked, beseeching him as was my custom when facing some great quandary.

But he provided no solution, not even the suggestion of one. He only rolled Thorn onto his stomach and stood over him with a contemptuous scowl. "There's nothing we can do; he has chosen this for himself."

"There must be something! A way to wake him up?"

"Until he decides to set aside this stupidity, there isn't."

The snap of his words made me draw back. "How can you be so cold, Father? After raising him as your own."

"Look at him, so lost in his ales he doesn't even know his wife and child have fled. It's pitiful. He is no son of mine. Not a man at all."

"Father…" Words escaped me. Despite the difficulties they'd had to overcome, he'd always loved Thorn as much as he did me. Sometimes moreso, I often teased when I came upon them sharing in some activity without me. To see him looking upon my cousin in such a way pierced through me as sure as a knife.

"You've seen he's alive," Father said, snatching up the lantern. "Let's return home. I'd like to go to bed."

He walked out of the kitchen, giving me no chance to argue further, and took with him our only source of light. I looked to Thorn again, never once having stirred despite our noisy presence, and my eyes filled.

What happened to you?

"Henrietta! We're leaving."

Without knowing what else to do and not wanting to stoke Father's ire further, I backed away and left my cousin facedown upon the floor.

Chapter Four

Birdie and Tabitha went back to the cottage the next morning, taken by Father with a basket of food in the gig.

Father and I had not spoken much during our walk back, and still, we did not address the previous night's venture when we met at the breakfast table after he'd made this second round trip and changed from his riding attire. He perused the weekly paper while Mother chatted idly about the ladies' garden society gathering she'd be attending that afternoon. So normal was the affair that it was as if we had not borne witness to Thorn's plight at all. Florence set the sideboard with servings of poached eggs, sausage, and toast with sides of marmalade and butter, along with apple slices and blackberries, a more generous spread than I'd become accustomed to, and I took only a small portion.

My stomach already felt full with sadness and the bites I managed were miniscule.

"Is this it, then?" I asked with my plate only half cleared.

"You'd like something else?" Mother perked up, ready to call Florence in with further instructions.

"We just pretend nothing's wrong?"

Father sighed from behind his paper and turned the page with a sharp crinkle. "Eat your breakfast."

"Last night—"

"Last night you saw the ramifications of poor choices, nothing more."

"But don't you think something must be troubling him?"

The paper came slamming down, his hand laid flat atop it. "What I *think* is that Thorn is a grown man, though I apply the term loosely, fully capable of making his own decisions. If something is troubling him, then he is responsible for handling it for the sake of those dependent upon him. What luxury it must be to live so recklessly, without care for anyone else. Had I, or my father or his father, done the same, do you think you'd be sitting here now, surrounded by every comfort imaginable? We've all faced hardship, but he should be given some special treatment because he refuses to rise above it?"

Where had Father seen this luxury he spoke of, I wanted to ask him, but Mother pushed away from the table with a napkin held to her mouth.

"Let us be finished with this," she said. "I can't listen to it anymore. My appetite is ruined."

After she'd gone, Father stared me down from the head of the table, and said in a way that brooked no further disagreement, "You will let this matter rest, Henrietta. We are already assisting your cousin as much as we can, providing him lodging and ensuring his family does not go without, though that seems of little concern to him. When he came to me initially, I opened my home to him without question for the second time in his life. This time, however, he squandered my goodwill on booze and debauchery, until I could abide it no longer. You did not see the way he raised his voice to your mother, *my wife*, or the mess he brought with him. He should count himself lucky he is still allowed on my land at all."

At the tremble of my lip, the hard lines upon his face softened into something more congenial. "You are always welcome here, my child; Daunderhead will forever be your home. But I will not allow you to continue to bother your mother so with this talk. Thorn is the only one who can help himself, and until he does, neither he, nor the issues he invites, will be welcome here again."

35

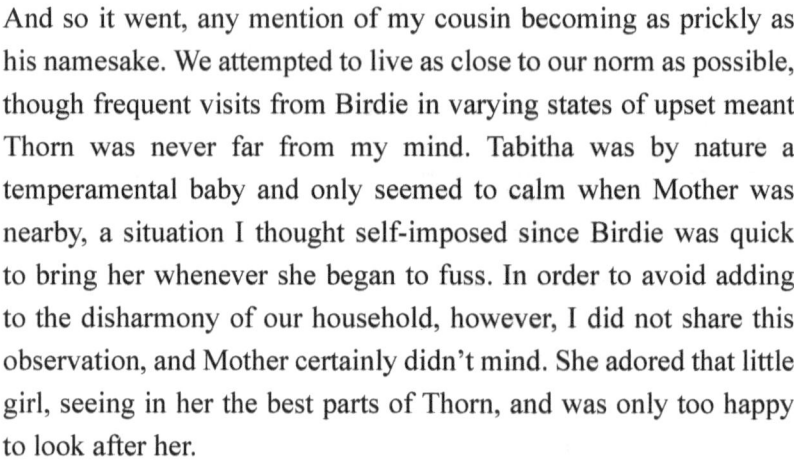

And so it went, any mention of my cousin becoming as prickly as his namesake. We attempted to live as close to our norm as possible, though frequent visits from Birdie in varying states of upset meant Thorn was never far from my mind. Tabitha was by nature a temperamental baby and only seemed to calm when Mother was nearby, a situation I thought self-imposed since Birdie was quick to bring her whenever she began to fuss. In order to avoid adding to the disharmony of our household, however, I did not share this observation, and Mother certainly didn't mind. She adored that little girl, seeing in her the best parts of Thorn, and was only too happy to look after her.

While Mother doted endlessly on her child, Birdie freely vented her frustration to me, explaining how Thorn accepted odd jobs around the village whenever he needed money to top up his stock, which embarrassed her greatly. Such unsteady employment was beneath our family station and would stir up unseemly questions and speculation. During these outings, he could sustain his sobriety, and when asked why he'd returned to Daunderhead, he'd make some claim about missing the fresh air and wanting to raise his daughter in the country way. Once behind closed doors in the evenings, however, he'd drink away his earnings. When his supply dwindled, he repeated the process.

To his credit, superficial as it may be, he kept his circumstances hidden, thus protecting Father's name and reputation.

I remained in my black, rising early each day for the onerous chore of ironing whichever of my two gowns I was to wear, much to Florence's chagrin. I assured her it would not reflect at all on her employment, which was to my knowledge faultless, and was only due to the habits I'd developed as a married woman without servants.

Truthfully, I needed to keep myself busy and sought to continue providing for myself as much as was deemed acceptable. Unable to attend or receive social calls under the rigorous expectations of a widow in deep mourning, I dined with my parents, took lengthy walks throughout the grounds, though never down a certain lane, and occupied my evenings with unserious novels and card games.

It was a pleasant facade, and for the sake of peace, I played into it.

Our fragile performance came to an end alongside Birdie's patience. After yet another moonlit walk to Daunderhead's front door, she wrote to her parents, requesting they wire funds for her and Tabitha's passage. She stated it was only a visit for Tabitha to know her side of the family, but was vague on the return details, "some weeks" down the line.

No one wondered why Thorn was not accompanying her.

Mother wept seeing them off and, without the frequent visits from Tabitha to brighten her moods, soon became withdrawn. I doubted my presence, still made melancholic at the slightest, most inconsequential provocation, provided her with much solace, however quick she was to dismiss my apologies. Father made every effort to cheer her, bringing her flowers, arranging luncheons, and bidding her to throw an autumn ball without any budgetary limit.

Mother simply could not muster enthusiasm for any of it.

The opposite of Father, she shouldered all blame for Thorn's drunkenness and wondered aloud if she had been a bad mother, negligent in some way, or perhaps too over-indulgent. Had she interfered too much in his family life, emasculating him as the head of his household, or not enough, leaving him without the proper guidance to navigate his roles? Whatever the scenario, she could find some way to manipulate it into being her fault.

37

She took to prayer, making frequent visits to church to ask God to release Thorn from the unholy grip upon him, and kept her Bible close at hand, referring to it often when her spirits were lowest.

Looking in on Thorn, often caught in some stage between contentious and inebriated, only made things worse.

"I'm taking your mother on holiday," Father said after she'd returned from a particularly horrible visit in which my cousin had been unable to speak or stand, only staring at her from under heavy, ringed lids.

She had come home and gone immediately upstairs to her bedroom, where she would not entertain Father or myself.

"Where?" I asked him, setting down the flowers I'd be rearranging from the selection he had half-filled our parlour with.

"A seaside resort hotel with a spa that boasts excellent healing properties. I've spoken to Dr. Coleshill and he agrees her health will only deteriorate if she continues in this way; the stress is too much for her. She needs the rich air and rest lest she develop hysteria. You will, of course, come with us."

Oh, how I wanted to accept. To stroll along the beach even without summer's heat and take in the salt and brine. How relaxing it would have been to step outside my own life and again adopt the airs of a young woman untroubled by bleak trends. These desires were tempered fast by guilt, for what right did I have to even imagine a public frolic while still clothed in crape?

"I can't," I said, gesturing to my veil and dress. "I've not even reached half-mourning yet. What would people think if they were to see me at a resort?"

He ruminated over this, stroking the length of his beard. "I have booked a grand suite already. You'd hardly need to leave."

"I appreciate the thought, but I really must decline. Here, I have all of Daunderhead to occupy me. A suite, no matter how grand, would seem a prison in comparison."

"I mean to take Florence with us. You will have no help."

"That's alright, I can sort my own cooking and cleaning."

"I don't like the thought of you alone," he said, unmollified.

"Thorn is not so far."

"I like the thought of him even less."

"Don't worry about me, Father." I laid my hand on his forearm with a gentle smile. "Take care of Mother."

To my surprise, Mother was even less amenable to the idea than I was. The timing was wrong, Birdie might return while they were away and need help with Tabitha, I shouldn't be left alone. All things centred around others that ignored her own well being and needs. Father nodded patiently to every excuse and then said, "We're going."

He gave her just days to grow used to the idea, knowing if she had more time it would only gnaw upon her nerves. I helped her pack, choosing gowns and dresses and the accoutrements to go with them to help build her excitement. My endeavour did serve its purpose to some degree, and by the morning of their departure, she even indicated she might be looking forward to their holiday.

Still, there were tears in her eyes as Father helped her and Florence into the carriage.

"You'll take care, won't you?"

"Yes, Mother," I replied.

"And you'll check on Thorn?"

"Goodness, Leonora, it's only two weeks," Father grumbled with good nature as he climbed in after her.

"Everything will be fine," I said, taking the hand she'd extended out to me.

After a reassuring squeeze, I stepped back to allow the carriage driver to close the door. Her expression through the window was one of trepidation, but Father said something that made her laugh, and the sight of her smile did gladden my heart.

I waved as the driver snapped his reins and stood upon the drive until I could no longer see the carriage, then went back inside to settle in the drawing room with tea and a book.

Daunderhead became a different place when it was all my own.

Its settling creaks took on a new tone, lower and longer lasting as if having to adjust to its emptiness. By afternoon, the overcast skies made for dreary lighting, painting each room with the sort of grey pallor that plays tricks on the eyes, deepening shadows and highlighting whites just enough to make the ordinary seem uncanny when caught on the edge of one's vision.

I decided rather quickly that I didn't need the whole of it open to me.

At my request, Florence had already drawn the curtains in the dining room, leaving only shadows to occupy the long table. I shut its doors, further closing it off, before walking down the hall to do the same to Father's office. The click of my heels upon the hardwood took on an echoing quality, and by imagination, gave the illusion I was being followed.

I laughed at the little thrill I'd given myself, having never inhabited the house alone, but knew without doubt that I had nothing to fear within my family home. With another, playful tap of my boot, I wandered further, to the billiard room, to continue my task.

I'd only meant to shut it as well, figuring I'd have little use for its games, but fond memories of running around the table with a stick as tall as I was pulled me in. Thorn had taught me to play, and how to lose, never fettering himself for the sake of my ego. Our laughter and fighting had filled those walls in equal measure when Father wasn't entertaining guests. It was also where Victor had found his footing with the Alden men, class providing no advantage behind the cue.

I trailed my fingers along the green baize bed, which blurred suddenly as tears welled.

Victor.

Thorn.

How did everything go so wrong?

I sank into one of the nearby armchairs and covered my face, suppressing the sobs that so desperately wanted to overtake me.

Why?

I asked myself that over and over until it was a scream inside my head.

Why Victor? Why Thorn?

Why Victor!

Why Thorn!

Why, Thorn?

My thoughts froze on that final question, turned accusatory. I could not ask God why He had seen fit to join me with my other half, only to rip him away and leave me forever unfinished. I would never know how my pain served His greater plan.

But, without Father there to stop me, I *could* confront my cousin.

Chapter Five

I do not know how I devised the plan that came next. It was so unlike myself, especially as someone who'd never developed a taste for alcohol, but when I spotted Father's liquor cabinet, I knew exactly how I wanted to approach Thorn.

I opened the glass panelled doors and surveyed the labelled bottles and crystal decanters. Having almost no knowledge of their contents, I lifted the top shelf's stoppers and sniffed before selecting the one that had been the most pleasing, which didn't amount to much when they all made my nose wrinkle. Based on my father's preferences, it was probably some port or brandy, but the specifics didn't matter.

I only needed it to be plentiful and palatable.

With the decanter held to my chest, I took leave of the billiard room and donned my cape for the walk to the cottage.

Thorn was not in when I arrived, but that did not stop me from entering. The stench of ale and old food belched forth at the door's opening. A blanket and pillow were left in an unmade heap on the sofa, hinting he had made this his bed. Getting up the steps was probably too challenging for him, and without Birdie there to goad him, he'd opted for convenience over propriety.

I grit my teeth, more determined now to follow through with my intentions, and perched on the armchair to await his return.

Whatever job he'd found that day must have been an involved one, keeping him longer than I anticipated. I grew restless in my waiting, made worse by breathing in the trapped malodors. What began as opening the windows to bring in fresh air turned into folding the blanket and then going to inspect the kitchen, where I discovered empty bottles, partially eaten food sprouting mould, and dirty clothing piled in a corner.

I stopped short of hauling in buckets of water to heat and fill the wash basin with, but only after scraping the dishes, clearing the bottles into a crate I'd found out the back door, and draping the clothes over the fence to help rid them of their bodied stink. I swept the floor free of debris and purged shelves of their rotting produce, throwing it as far from the cottage as possible for wildlife to feast on. With the table cleared and wiped free of crumbs and damp spots, I placed the decanter down and removed the stopper.

My hands clenched into a joined fist, fingertips kneading flesh. Second thoughts dredged to the surface, roused by my idleness. Was it truly my place to accost Thorn in the manner I'd so hastily conceived? How would he react? The temper he'd developed was no secret, but how severely would he turn it on me? There was still time for me to retreat, although there would be no denying I'd been there.

I silenced the overlapping doubts with a swig from the decanter that burned all the way down to my belly. I sputtered, grimacing at the harsh flavour, and rubbed my chest to soothe the lingering smoulder.

None of this would be easy, that was all the more evident now, but I had come with a purpose and I meant to see it through.

I had taken more sips by the time I heard the clink of glass outside and the front door open. Thorn's footsteps faltered on the threshold, driven to pause by the tidiness he'd not left, then his voice called out, "Hello? Aunt Leonora?"

43

That he assumed it had been my mother's work and not his wife's doing rankled me, an annoyance that was both mine and whet by the drink. His first thought should have been for his bride, followed by exhilaration at their possible reunion, but he had so resigned himself to sorry fate that it did not even cross his mind as an option.

"Here," I said, emboldened with liquid courage.

The bottles sounded again, tapping softly together as Thorn shifted, hesitating for a moment before he slowly crossed into the kitchen.

He entered to me sitting at the table, illuminated against the descending dusk by a single candle, reminiscent of the night Father and I had found him on the floor, though he would have no memory of that. He was clean now, his hair still too long, but combed into a sensible style, and any stains on his shirt were hidden beneath a waistcoat and jacket. Something that wasn't meant to last if the eight-bottle crate in his arms was any indication.

For the moment, though, he was sober.

Good. I wanted him alert.

He set the crate down and removed his bowler with the slowness of an off-guard man, laying it atop his ale like it might hide his sin. "What are you doing here?"

"I've been home for a while now."

"I know; I'd been told. I meant–"

"And you never once came to inquire after me?" I could feel heat already rising to my face, the anger I'd continued to harbour and let fester in my darkest recesses beginning to alight.

"I–" he frowned, gaze moving to the open decanter in front of me. "Are you drinking?"

I slapped the table and my drink splashed in its crystal as I pushed myself up. "Sit, dear cousin."

"What's going on, Netta? If Uncle sees you like this–"

The room seemed to tilt ever so slightly, just enough for my feet to slide unsteadily beneath me, but I made it to him and forced him by the shoulders into a chair. Shock made him compliant and he allowed my rough ministrations before I returned to the seat across from him.

"Let me bring you home," he said, but I raised my voice over his.

"You will do no such thing! You, Thorn Alden, will sit there and you will watch."

"I don't know what you're trying to do here except make a fool of yourself."

My laughter was like the bray of a donkey. "Then I am off to the ideal start! For I have come to be your reflection."

He did not speak then, his mouth drawn so tight in a dour line as understanding took hold. But I did not need, nor want, him to say anything. I lifted the decanter to him in mocking cheer and swallowed another mouthful. It went down smoother the more I drank and the burn had turned to a pleasant warmth that extended into my limbs.

"So much of my time has been spent on you since I arrived. Did you know that? No, you couldn't, could you? Drowning so deep in your cups you had no idea who was coming or going. Do you know what it's been like? Do you even care?" I leaned far over the table and snapped my fingers in front of his face. "Listen to me! Listen, and look at me to see yourself. This is what you've become!"

Again I pulled from the decanter and he averted his eyes, staring sidelong at the wall while his fingers drummed an agitated beat against his knee.

Meanwhile, my words continued to pour from me, growing louder, becoming barbed. "You made it so you didn't have to see Mother's worry or share the weight of new parenthood with Birdie. After losing your job, your home, both forgivable, you couldn't even

45

be there for them! You still had everything that truly meant something! Why would you risk that? Why would you give it up? All for what?"

He did not even try to answer.

I was on my feet again, my cheeks wet with furious tears, and I lunged at his crate in so swift a move it surprised both of us. I didn't know what I was going to do until I had my grip round the nearest bottle's neck.

"What I would not give for one more minute with Victor! To have had a family with him!" I stared down at the bottle in my grasp, breath wild. "The very thing you trade so willingly. Why?"

The smash of the bottle against the wall punctuated my question.

Thorn leapt up, but I threw another and mine was a short lived gallows smile when it too shattered.

"Stop!"

"Then tell me!" I screamed, hoisting a third. "The Thorn I knew, the one I named my brother, would never have behaved like this. Why now?"

He stood stiffly, muscles bound in tense coils, and the snarl on his face was unlike anything I'd ever seen. I shrieked when he batted his chair so hard aside it crashed against the wall and lunged at me, forcing me to cower against the cupboards while he loomed above me, teeth bared.

"Shut up, you rooting sow!"

How quickly my anger was snuffed out by his roar. Although tremors of fear stirred within, they were secondary to the forlorn anchor dragging my heart down. Through the veil of inebriation, I had yet hoped I would spark something in Thorn. Some remorse or an awakening. By forcing him to view the antics of a drunkard up close, I thought he might renounce his ways and return to his prior self.

It had clearly been the belief of a naive girl with more love in her than logic.

The bottle slipped from my fingers, suddenly slack with despair, and I lifted my bleary eyes to his, whispering, "What happened to you?"

He reared back, arm raised to strike, and I hugged myself, bracing with my features twisted into an expectant flinch. A vein in his forehead throbbed and spittle dotted his lips. His fist shook in the air.

"No," he growled through teeth clenched so tight they appeared on the verge of breaking.

Thorn did swing, but his aim was high, and struck hard upon the wall with a reverberating crack. I drew in a sharp breath, and by instinct almost reached for his hand to check for injury, but something flickered across the whole back of it then, like the sheen of a web caught just so in the light, visible for only an instant.

I went still, raised fingers curling slowly closed, and fixated on the blood seeping in beads from his knuckles.

"You shouldn't be here," he said with none of the vitriol that infused his words before and turned away from me.

The floor rolled under my feet and I stumbled past him to my chair, stomach lurching into my throat and doubling me over. I was relieved when I did not express myself then and there, though the threat of it hung as a guillotine over my head.

"Come, I'll walk you home."

He sounded so weary, an abrupt change in hardly the blink of an eye. That, combined with the strange ripple upon his hand, sloshed around in my booze-laden brain as formless thoughts, slipping just beyond comprehension. All I could decipher of them was an inclination, though I had not the wherewithal to figure out what was driving it or how to explain it were I able to try.

I only knew that something was wrong.

The small hairs along my arms rose, bristling at this keen certainty wedged at the forefront of my awareness.

"Thorn?"

I picked up my head, nearer to a block of lead than a skull, and looked at him through the candle's bobbing flame. He stood in the archway between kitchen and main room, outlined with his arms crossed in the weak orange glow.

And shrouded in the dark that flooded the cottage beyond, a line of silhouettes formed a half-circle at his back.

Ranging drastically in height, they spasmed in subtle jerks and twitches that quivered down bent limbs and crooked necks. Utter silence surrounded them as if all sound had been swallowed by their presence, and my pounding heart filled it with its quickening beat.

I shoved away from the table so violently that the decanter toppled and its contents spilled unchecked in an amber puddle. Thorn gaped, puzzled, then following my terrified stare, his eyes went wide. He rushed to me and took me by the wrist to drag me out the rear door. Fear and liquor worked in conjunction to turn my flight clumsy and I stumbled in his wake, craning to see if those terrible spectres were following.

We whipped around the side of the cottage and onto the lane without further sighting, but it did not slow Thorn, who charged ahead, never once looking back as I so frequently did.

"You saw them too," I gasped once my tongue unknotted itself.

He did not answer, nor did he relent our breakneck pace through the open country toward Daunderhead.

I collapsed in the foyer after he thrust me across the threshold, head swimming, stomach churning, unable to catch my breath. My cousin sank against the doorway, mouth hanging open to take in gulps of air.

"Thorn," I cried plaintively between pants. "What were those?"

His eyes flicked to me, then back to the starry sky. "There was nothing."

"There was! I know you saw them too."

"You're drunk."

"Then explain what caused you to flee your own home like that?"

"You did," he said. "You would not go otherwise, you made that very clear."

But I shook my head. "You're lying!"

"Listen to me, Netta: Stay away. It's for the best. Now fetch some water and go to bed. You will regret all of this tomorrow."

"Please," I crawled after him in a most undignified display and took hold of his sleeve. "Stay here. Don't go back. You know I speak the truth. There was something there and it was *wrong*."

I could not read his expression as he unfastened my fingers from his arm and slumped back on my heels. "Thorn."

"Stop," he said softly, and I caught sight of the brother I'd thought lost, caring and gentle, but so burdened it smothered the light within him. "Go to bed and forget this."

I redoubled my effort, desperate to hold on to that glimpse. A sob grew like a cherry pit in my throat. "Come in, stay! I'll make tea. We can play billiards like we used to. Father isn't here, you don't need to worry about him."

But Thorn backed away, pulling the door closed after him.

"Goodnight, Netta."

Chapter Six

I stayed curled on the floor where Thorn left me for a long while, pinned by the weight of grief and the queasiness that roiled at the slightest movement. The cool wood was welcome against my cheek, though it did no favours to the rest of me, and my neck developed a terrible cramp that at last made me haul myself upright. With only the moon's natural light to soften the dark and my usual surefooting sorely affected, I held my arms out and teetered to the stairs.

I *had* seen things, I thought as I used the bannister to pull myself up steps made narrow and tilting.

Not things.

People.

Or something similar to people, anyway. The way they had moved, those little twitches, had not been like any I'd seen another person make. And the silence, so devoid of life. I shuddered at the memory of it. Surely I was not capable of concocting something so grotesque, even under the influence of Father's liquor cabinet. And Thorn's reaction had not been one of irritation. There had been fear there.

Hadn't there?

As I staggered down the hall, feeling my way along the wall, I tried to replay the minutes leading up to our mad dash and the exact look upon his face. First came that terrible expression, seething with hateful malice that turned him a stranger. Dwelling too long on it weakened my knees, both from the fright he'd evoked in me and the knowledge he was capable of becoming that person at all. I pushed my way past his snarling visage, focusing instead on his sudden shift and what had come after. Wide eyes, of that much I was certain. But I had just knocked the decanter over, hadn't I? Was it possible I'd misread his surprise as something else to better match what I'd been feeling? If that was indeed the case, then he might have really only wanted to be rid of me. It still did not explain why he had forced us to run all the way to Daunderhead.

None of it made sense, but I was in no state for deep deductive reasoning.

I made it into my room and slouched against the closed door, my palm cupped to my forehead in attempt to lessen the throbbing that was building alongside the questions. What an abject failure my intervention had been, leaving me sick from overindulgence and Thorn angry with me. Desiring to leave the entire wretched event behind me, I fell face down on my bed without so much as kicking off my boots.

I wished only to sleep.

It was difficult to drift off, however, when the room felt as if it were spinning even with my eyes closed. I clutched my bedding with a groan and cursed whatever Devil drink I'd been unlucky enough to consume. Despite my misery, I did eventually curl up in such a way that minimised the sensation, and sleep crept closer.

With consciousness only a tenuous thing, I did not pay any heed to the first knock coming from further down the hall, closer to Mother's chambers. It was a weak sound, one I dismissed as some usual house noise made in the late hours. The slow shuffle after was likewise disregarded.

Even when the knock repeated with the three, faint thuds closer by, I was too wrapped in near slumber to consider it seriously. The alcohol haze made everything seem so separate from me as if it were occurring far and away, beyond my worry. I was at last comfortable and all felt but a dream.

I only curled up tighter when the floorboards outside my room creaked, and thrice the same knock came, this time upon my door.

51

"*Mercy*," a shivering whisper begged. "*Please. Mercy.*"

But I was already slipping away, and it echoed in the dark descent to sleep.

It was either the migraine or birdsong that woke me, both so unpleasant that I moaned long and low into my blankets. Sunlight filled the room as an unwelcome guest, only worsening the stabbing pain behind my eyes. By its brightness, I figured I had missed most of the early morning if not all of it entirely.

Getting out of bed was a chore unlike any I'd undertaken since the first morning I woke without Victor beside me. The figure that met me in the mirror was still clothed in yesterday's wrinkled dress, with her hair falling from its twists and her face creased with the quilt's embroidery. I considered trying to salvage some of my respectability before leaving the privacy of my chamber, but merely undressing sounded too gruelling a task, and besides, there was no one else in the house to judge me. Before I could handle so arduous an undertaking as removing my clothing, I decided that first I needed to assuage the symptoms of my deviance.

Making it down the steps to the kitchen was a most precarious affair. There, with a wince at every sound and eyes squeezed into an afflicted squint, I was able to pull my wits together enough to brew a cup of feverfew tea to treat my head and fry bread in fat to soak up the remnants of my mistake, a remedy taught to me by my late husband.

My condition made eating a slow process, wherein every bite had to be thoroughly chewed and washed down with the tea. It gave me ample time to revisit the night before, though much of it was spent in self-debate over what was accurate memory and what was my imagination's attempt to fill in gaps.

Mercy.

The single phrase floated upward, but everything around it was murky. I turned it over in my mind, stretched it out, tried to fit it into various points of the evening. Had I said it? I didn't think so, though with what I recalled of Thorn's actions, it wouldn't have been unwarranted. However I had come by it, there was something in it that had hooked itself in my consciousness and refused to come loose.

"Mercy," I whispered, gazing into the almost empty tea cup.

No clearer vision was afforded to me and I drained the rest in a single swig, chasing it with the last of the toast. Still quite miserable, I abandoned the kitchen and the dirty dishes I'd created and went back upstairs to fetch my dressing gown.

Nothing sounded more appealing than a hot bath to further treat my ailments and I went straight to Mother's suite to put its lavish clawfoot tub to use. Once the water was running at a steaming temperature, I plugged the drain and stood before the mirror, plucking out the pins that held resolutely in my hair. Once I'd shaken the mass of curls free and worked through the larger knots, I went again to the tub, now half full, and knelt beside it to run my fingers along its surface. Already I could feel my muscles relaxing and my gaze strayed to the window over the tub, hand trailing absently back and forth while I waited for it to fill to my satisfaction.

As I danced my fingers through the water, humming softly some nameless tune, something soft brushed against their tips.

I jerked my hand back with a gasp and held it up in shock. Water drops rolled down my wrist and dampened my cuff, but they went unnoticed, for around the end of my thumb was caught a strand of golden hair. A colour not found on anyone in Daunderhead. I clamoured upright with a shudder, wiping it hurriedly against my skirt, and looked inadvertently into the tub in my rush to turn off the tap.

A cloud of yellow tendrils floated like seaweed within the rippling water. My heart skipped and a strangled exclamation escaped me, but my legs had become locked, useless, held hostage by fascinated horror. The hair bobbed gently as if pushed by impossible currents, and its thick lengths were drawn slightly apart, enough for the sliver of a greyed face to become visible. Its skin was sallow, holding no true colour, and blackened holes with ragged edges bore through the flesh as if eaten away. Teeth gleamed where the corner of the upper lip should have been, and the nose was an open cavity.

But nothing was so awful as the eye.

It stared upward from an unlidded socket, swollen and pale as a peeled grape. Trapped within its centre, dilated into an inky pool, was such helpless terror that it stole my breath, taking with it the scream lodged in my throat.

Until that eye flicked suddenly to me.

I broke out into a shriek that must have filled the whole house and turned for the door, but the water erupted in a drenching spray, and fingers entangled in my loose hair, forcing my head back. Bony arms riddled with barnacle pustules wrapped around my neck and it latched itself to me. Its touch was ice, leeching all warmth from me, and from it wafted the stench of rotting fish and low tide. Its mouth stretched open in a keen that rivalled mine, elongating the tears shorn into its cheeks, and it dragged me with it into the bath.

Only the lower half of my legs remained above the water, turned frothy by my panicked struggles. I clawed at the arms clutching so tight, nails slashing through the papery skin with ease, but it held fast, scrabbling to maintain its grasp. We rolled and pitched in desperate throes that saw me completely submerged. Like the barnacles encrusting its limbs, it refused to be shaken. On the contrary, all my floundering only seemed to make it constrict tighter, squeezing the last reserves from my lungs.

My body shook for want of air and the edges of my vision, filled with those golden tresses, wavered. I gripped the edge of the tub and wrenched myself as far upright as I was able, managing for only a moment to break through the surface.

My mother's bathroom was gone. In the fleeting seconds, my head was above water, it was to an endless expanse of slate sea. My lungs filled with frigid salt air that in turn burned my eyes and I wasted it on another scream that trailed after me when I was again yanked beneath the crashing waves.

It was only my white knuckled grip on porcelain that kept me from giving over completely to hysteria. Regardless of what I thought I'd seen, there could be no denying I was still in my family home, in the tub, so long as I didn't let go. I thrashed still but could feel myself becoming weaker. So desperate to breathe, my mouth opened of its own accord to a rush of hot water impossibly tinged with brine. I saw white, I thought in white, all I heard was a shrill whistle, like a train bearing down on me, but behind it lurked a dangerous calm, edging away the panic, easing me toward stillness. It invited me to let go of the dread and merely float. My fingers loosened on the tub's edge.

All at once, the weight vanished from 'round my neck and my face burst free of the bath. That first draw of breath reignited my terrified frenzy. I flailed with wheezing cries, slapping at the surface, and heaved myself over the side of the tub to crash in a sopping heap upon the floor. The dye ran from my crape trim and left a streak of black upon the tiles after me as I scrambled for the door, coughing and shouting hoarsely for help that was not there.

In the hallway, I could not resist the urge to look over my shoulder in case of pursuit. The tub's remaining water, left a dirty grey by my dress, benignly lapped its sides. No blonde hair, nor the horrid thing beneath it, were visible in its shallow depths. All was as it should be save for the far spread splashes.

But for the steam, still hanging, mist-like, over the stained and soaked room, and its subtle scent of a far off sea.

Chapter Seven

Nothing had ever scared me in Daunderhead. Not the wind and rain lashing against windows on stormy nights, no shadowed corner or creaking floorboard. It was home, and home was always safe. Even as a girl, my parents and grandparents had instilled such a sense of belonging that I believed I merely had to politely ask any wayward spirits to leave me alone and they would be bound to listen by virtue of my family's ownership.

Daunderhead Hall had always been the Aldens'. It knew us the same way we knew it and we took care of one another. Grandmother in particular believed in the house's spirit, that it formed and grew based on those within it. A strong family formed strong bones that would protect it and weather any element.

But as I ran down the hall with my wet skirt gathered in my arms and sobs cutting like glass shards in my raw throat, I knew fear. I tasted its copper upon my tongue, felt its vice squeezing tighter and tighter so every breath was but a gasp.

Even in my room, always my domain and under my control, it followed, seeping in through the crack beneath my door and making me question every curtain flutter and darkened space. I tore at my dress, suddenly strangled by its water-logged weight, and kicked it away. It landed heavily in a pile, one sleeve flung askew, and I could just imagine it beginning to rise, filling out and taking the form of that rotting, golden haired creature until it was standing before me in my own mourning, foetid hands outstretched for my throat.

Horrified by such a vision, I spun for my wardrobe and snatched the nearest undergarments and dress.

I fled Daunderhead, hair undone, my garments sticking to still damp skin, and I ran with all I had down the heather-lined lane until my heart was throwing itself against my chest and the wind had been replaced with blood rushing in my ears. The quiet country unfurled around me, spreading in such vibrant colours that every painter's palette would envy. I took no pleasure in the afternoon sun or the way it played upon the trees and fields. I did not stop to lean against the low stone wall to admire distant flocks of sheep. There would be none of my usual dalliances. There was only a single place I could think to go.

I stumbled the last few steps to Thorn's door, gasping for breath and dripping perspiration, and pounded upon it with a closed fist.

"Thorn!"

I gave him no time before barging in, but hardly had to walk inside before locating my cousin. He was sitting on the floor, his back against the sofa and his chin lolled to his chest. The bottles I hadn't broken the night before stood sentry around him, drained of their innards, and between his legs was propped the crystal decanter, empty as the rest. His eyes did not so much as flutter with the banging of the door, though his snoring might well have drowned it out. I uttered a desperate cry and ran to him, shaking him by his shirt front as fiercely as I could. His head rolled to one side, but it was an unconscious movement driven by my rattling.

"Please, please, please, wake up," I begged into his face, delivering a rapid series of taps upon his cheek. When still he did not rouse, they graduated to hard slaps.

Thorn groaned, one arm jumped slightly in what might have been an attempt to brush me away, but that was all I could get from him. His breath reeked of alcohol so strongly he must have only finished it a short while ago.

I stood with a disgusted, shaking sigh and stepped over him, knocking over some of his glass guard. I stopped myself from reaching down to pick them up, deciding in my distress that he deserved to awaken surrounded by his folly. I was not brave enough to leave him, however, for even in such a state, his presence supplied just enough fortitude to keep me in my faculties. I dropped into the easy chair and pulled my legs beneath me, too skittish to allow them to dangle before its underside.

Prickles dotted up and down my arms, fear and cold entwining to quash any sense of reprieve I might have found outside of Daunderhead. I did not have a name for the thing that attacked me, nor an explanation for how it came to be in my mother's tub. I kept seeing its eye fixating on me, unblinking and bulging, its lid torn away. I thought I might drown in the memory of its abyssal pupil as surely as I almost had in the bathwater. I hugged myself, nails digging into my upper arms, and rocked with rapid, whispered prayers to dispel the horror from my head.

They cracked into quiet pleas for aid, directed first at God, then turned on Thorn. If either heard me, they both remained silent.

"Am I going mad?" I asked my slumbering cousin, looking helplessly to him. "Is this a woman's frailty plaguing me? Losing Victor, you...I fear heartbreak is beginning to divorce me from what's real. If I were to tell you what just happened to me, you would agree and send for my parents' return at once."

But the black stains upon my skin left by weeping crape belied this as the whole truth. So too did the tenderness of my neck where arms had coiled and pulled. I grazed my throat with a featherlight touch. I could not have done that to myself.

"It was a waking nightmare," I continued softly, devolving into a scattered ramble. "Something attacked me. It was almost a person, a woman, I think, but so horrible she was nearer a monster. Cold as the grave, missing whole chunks of flesh, and her eye. The way she looked at me. And there was an ocean, she took me there, though I don't know how. We were in Mother's bathtub, then we weren't." I buried my face in my hands, nearly sick at reliving it over again. "Oh, I don't know! You'd laugh if you could hear me. You'd tell me I'd been reading too much again. But I swear, Thorn, this is what happened."

He did not laugh. There came no fond rebuke. He only slept the drunkard's sleep, impervious to my plight.

I wanted to hate him then, to turn all the fury and fright that bellowed within me upon him and yell until there was not enough alcohol in the world to shield him from my wrath. I wanted to lay my blame as stones upon his chest. Birdie's departure, his daughter's absence, Father's anger, Mother's sorrow. I could have even found a way to pin Victor's demise on him if I'd put half a mind to it.

If I'd not looked at him and seen in his face the young boy who had been my first dance partner, leading me in exaggerated steps across the floor to make me giggle while our instructor admonished him. The one who had sat in the drawing room with me and teased me endlessly about my poor piano playing, only to sit down and bang recklessly upon the keys while insisting *this* was how it was meant to be done. The one who, upon learning of my engagement, sent a congratulatory correspondence that ended with a note to Victor:

She shall be your problem now, but always my sister.

Below, he had painstakingly sketched a boot alongside a carrot, which had befuddled Victor enormously. He had shown it to me, only becoming more confused at my peals of laughter.

"What does it mean, Netta?" he'd asked with a grin.

"It's quite rude," I giggled. "I shouldn't say."

But he had cajoled and tickled until I decoded the crude hieroglyphs, explaining Thorn was fond of saying that if a man were to cross me, he'd correct him with a well placed carrot inserted via a swift kick. Ever after, wagging a carrot at one another was a playful warning between us, moments made possible by my cousin.

Softened by reminiscence, I climbed from my chair and picked up the bottles and decanter, setting them on the desk to get them off the floor. Then, still afflicted by a chill, I went outside to fetch logs from the pile and found only scrap wood left. Very little of it was useful, but I gathered enough to build a decent fire in the hearth. Once it was crackling pleasantly, I took the blanket from the sofa and draped it across Thorn.

I could never hate him, I knew as I tucked it around his shoulders, but my soul ached at loving him while he tore down the life he'd worked so hard to build, every bottle another brick gone.

Weary through and through, I lay on the sofa behind him, knees curled to my stomach, and stared at the flames, allowing their hypnotic dance to lull me to uneasy rest.

The fire had dimmed to embers by the time I awoke to a cottage doused in night's black. Its lingering flickers cast long, writhing shadows along the walls that, in my unfocused gaze, took on human-like shapes with arms upraised and heads turning. I told myself it was only from the furniture, nothing more fantastic, and stopped my pensive chewing upon my lower lip. Thorn was where I had left him, his snores reduced to deep, rumbling breaths, which helped ease the unravelling of my nerves. I stretched in an arch and rolled onto my back with a tired sigh, hoping the ceiling would be free of anything that might further spark my overly excitable mind.

That excitement soon frosted over. Without the fire, the temperature had dropped significantly, leaving me with chattering teeth that worsened the longer I lay there. I considered taking back the blanket I'd laid over Thorn but knew the resulting guilt would have me returning it before the cold had a chance to rouse him.

As I debated going upstairs to take a covering from his bed, a drawn out creak permeated the dark.

I went rigid as it trailed into pregnant silence, breath caught behind now clenched teeth, and looked out of the corner of my eyes to the sofa back. The sound had come from somewhere over it, by the stairs, blessedly blocked from my view.

No sooner had it ended than it repeated, the lethargic groans carrying on in a dull vibrato, accompanied by the roll of rockers over stone flooring.

The rocking chair.

It never found a steady rhythm, pitching back and forth at a disjointed, languid pace, sometimes pausing for an eternity of seconds, then resuming its uneven intervals. Back and forth, back and forth, as if to the very front tip of its rockers, then so far back I thought it might fall over. And with each pass, another prolonged creak, ominous as a clock's tick in the Reaper's wake.

Layered beneath the grating of the chair was a rasping hiss, just as laboriously produced, that I did not immediately recognize as breathing. It crackled with every inhale and was expelled as a thin sigh as if merely holding breath was too great a burden.

The cottage did become so small then, the space between my person and that chair only an arm's length apart, kept separate by the low back of the sofa. If I so much as propped myself up on an elbow, I would be visible to anything behind it. A claustrophobic churn began in my belly, sending waves of panic crashing outward.

I pressed myself as deeply into the sofa's cushion as I could, eyes clamped so tightly closed, and I mouthed prayers to Lord Jesus to banish whatever spectre now loomed. I did not stop until the rocking did, ending on a long series of stuttered creaks that faded into silence. The breathing also ceased with a wilting exhale, but I continued to pray into the quiet for many minutes more until I had the courage to crack open one eye.

The fire had died further, masking much of the room. I reassured myself that Thorn was still at my side by reaching out and touching him upon the shoulder, a solid affirmation I was desperate for. Mouth dry from terror, I glanced to the kitchen, only a few meagre steps away, and listened once more. When mine was the only breathing I heard, I slid my legs over the side of the sofa and began to stand.

The rocking chair creaked, and I whirled towards it.

Spider webbing red, like cracks of glowing ember over black, wove across the seated figure, travelling up and across its entire body. There were no features to speak of, lost both to shadow and char, only scorched flesh around a mouth stretched to painful limits. It began to lift its hand with fingers reduced to gnarled stumps, palm up as if entreating me.

I yelped, backing rapidly away, and in doing so, tripped over Thorn's outstretched legs. As I fell, the smouldering figure released a wounded, croaking howl.

Chapter Eight

I added my scream in shrill chorus and wrapped my arms around my head, sure it was going to come 'round the sofa after me. When the expected grasp closed on my forearm, I kicked with both feet and pummelled upon its back with my free fist, my scream turning to a frantic squeal.

"Netta!"

"Thorn?"

My eyes popped open to my cousin's bloodshot eyes level with mine. I launched myself at him, clinging to his neck with full-body sobs.

"Why are you here?" he asked, arms hanging limp at his sides.

"Something's wrong. With me, or Daunderhead, I don't know, but I have seen terrible things!"

"What?"

"Spectres! Maybe demons? I cannot say with any certainty for I've never encountered their like before."

"More than one?"

"Two. A woman in the bath and here, just now, an awful, burned creature. It was sitting in the rocking chair right over there."

I pointed emphatically, but when I got to my feet, pulling Thorn up after me, it was only to an empty seat. Thorn's brow furrowed into a frown.

"Wait," I exclaimed, grabbing his wrist again as if it would better help my spotty memory. "There was another, I think. Last night, I believed it might have been a dream, but there was knocking and a voice. It was saying...mercy."

When he only tugged himself free, I begged, "Please, do not dismiss me."

He made a muffled sound in the back of his throat and, with fingers pressed to temple, searched the room until he found the bottles lined up on the desk. He lifted them, gave each a little shake, and having confirmed they were empty, set them down with increasingly frustrated firmness.

"What are you doing?"

"I need a drink."

I baulked at him with a disbelieving scoff. "Have you heard a single thing I've said?"

"There should've been more," he muttered as if I hadn't spoken.

"Oh, I'm sure you made up for the three bottles I broke and then some with the liquor I left."

"There was hardly any still in it."

"As if that's the point! If you won't listen to me, then at least listen to yourself," I snapped. "I'm standing before you, telling you something is happening to me, and all you care about is crawling back into a bottle. You aren't even completely sober yet!"

Stiffness stretched across his shoulders and he scowled downward. "I don't expect you to understand."

"I want to!" I cried. "Every day I have asked myself what happened to you to make you this way. I'd have asked you as well, but if you're not already in your cups, you're out looking for ways to refill them."

"I'm fine."

"Are you? Is any of this? Have you even noticed that everyone else is gone? You're all I have and I can't even rely on you!"

"An incredible act, cousin, coming in as if your concern lies with me, but how you reveal yourself," he said without malice, words flat. "I apologise for the effect this is having on you."

"That's not what I meant."

"Regardless," he said, going to the armchair, where he sat with elbows upon his knees and his fingers curled beneath his chin. "I am sorry."

"I don't want you to be sorry; I want you to stop!" I said, voice lifting, impassioned by his indifference.

"I told you I'm fine."

"For God's sake, be a man, Thorn!"

"Listen to me," he said, tone unchanging, staring at some unfixed point in front of him. "What you think you've seen–"

"What I *know* I've seen!"

"Pay it no heed. For your own good, let it lie. Go home. Do not come back here."

"What do you mean 'let it lie'?" His words cast a pall over me, one of dangerous suggestion that cooled my temper. I knelt at his feet and tried to make him face me. "What are you talking about?"

"Just know it is not your concern."

"I was attacked! I could have been killed. Of course it's my concern."

He hesitated, throat bobbing with agitation. He looked everywhere but at me. "You'll be fine, I promise."

The dying fire made hollows of his eyes and I wrapped my hands over his, trying to return some warmth to him. "Whatever this is, we can take it together, like we always have. Tell me what you know. I can help."

His jaw tightened into a taut glower that went over my shoulder.

"Just talk to me," I insisted.

A ripple ran across his features at my prompting, like the barest glint of sunlight reflecting off the surface of a pond. His frown curled into a sardonic sneer. "You can help?" he scoffed in a scratchy mimic of my voice. "I don't need help. What I need is for you to stop meddling."

"Meddling in what?"

"There you go again," he spat, gripping the armrests and jutting forward with his arms angled out. "Always sticking your nose in."

65

I shied away from the venom infused in his tone. "Thorn, you're frightening me."

"You're frightened, are you?"

"Stop this at once!"

He exploded upward with such ferocity that I fell onto my backside, hands raised in defence. He slapped them aside and snarled his fingers in my hair, yanking me further off balance.

"I don't take orders from no tart!"

I shrieked, scratching at him and trying to twist out of his grasp, but he dragged me across the floor and threw me into a wall. He came away with strands of my hair still tangled around his fingers. I crumpled, whimpering and clasping my throbbing scalp, paralyzed by complete and petrified astonishment.

"Nobody never taught you your proper place," he growled. He had me by the bodice front, pinned to the wall with his fist driven into my collarbone. He needled it further, grinding bone upon bone until I cried out. "It's time you learned."

Thorn hauled me up roughly. My head snapped to the side with the blow delivered across my cheek by the back of his hand and I screamed for him to stop.

"Seems you're a slow learner, ain't you?"

He pulled back for another hit and I reached out to curl my fingers in the collar of his shirt.

"Are you going to beg?" he asked with a wolfish grin, all teeth and no amity.

Tightening my hold, I stared up at him, and brought my knee up as swiftly and as hard as I could, cracking it against his manhood. His eyes flew wide, snide expression vanishing into a colour-drained gape, and my knee found its mark a second time, following through with the lesson Thorn himself had provided so many years before.

How to hit. Where. And never just once.

He went to his knees, hands cupped betwixt his legs, and I booted him in the stomach, toppling him completely. While he dribbled curses and saliva, I darted for the door and ran.

Tears obscured the dark path and I veered this way and that, staggering on quaking legs. Overgrowth snatched at my skirt hem, but I lacked the wherewithal to carry it any higher, and rocks seemed to sprout from the ground to get caught beneath my boots and hinder my retreat. An owl's lament haunted the brisk wind travelling down from the hills, a mere bird call at any other time, but then it rang as an ill portent.

The laneway shifted, curving through a section of creeping thistle and close growing trees. As I ran past a thick patch, mere outlines of stalks and blooms in the moonlight, something closed around my ankle and pulled the ground from under me. I crashed down with a startled cry and, ignoring the sting in my knee where I'd landed upon a stone, rolled at once to my back to look down my leg.

It was not by the moon that I saw the hand, coming from beneath a cart and clamped like a shackle just above my foot. Gas lamps arced over a cobbled street that I had just traversed as a dirt path. Open country had been replaced with brick and mortar, closing me in between buildings that left only a smudge of sky overhead. The stink of urine burned in my nostrils, stronger than the mingling whiffs of overlapping suppers and horses.

Like the ocean in the bathtub all over again.

"No," I exhaled softly, heart hammering.

I tried to shove away from the cart, but whatever had me refused to be shaken. Its fingers, so pale as to be almost blue, flexed with my effort, their hold unbroken. In the darkness beneath the cart, dragging weight scraped over cobblestone. A second hand emerged, shorn nails splintering further as it pulled itself forward with agonising feebleness, trying to come fully out into the open. With a starkly uttered gasp, I brought up my captured leg and slammed it into the ground, drawing from the hand's owner a burbling moan, but still, it refused to relent. Heaving itself on its belly, it slid forward, breaking from cover.

Wet red glistened in the dim lamplight overhead, pouring in rivulets down his face from an ugly wound split from eyebrow to ear tip. A depression sank the middle of his skull inward, and in its valley, fleshy matter stuck out between blood matted hair. He was barely out of boyhood, perhaps not even old enough to have shared his first proper kiss. His features were gaunt, eyes sunken into black rings, teeth fragmented, nose splayed sideways across his cheek. He made a sound as if attempting to speak, but only blood and tooth shards came out.

I was not so silent, and my horror wrested from my lips to fill the city street.

In my feverish attempts to escape, my heel caught him across the chin, then, more pointedly, in the throat. He vomited a stream of red upon my boot, but it had the desired effect and his grip loosened enough for me to wriggle free. I stumbled away, half crawling on hands and knees, breath coming quick and ragged.

"Help!" I screamed, wondering how not one window had come alive with curious eyes attracted by the racket.

But my entreaty went only to a thick patch of thistle and close growing trees.

I wheeled around with a bark of delirious laughter that evaporated in an instant. He was lying across the path behind me, ruined face craned upwards, staring at me. His moan was a wounded animal's. I backed away in shuffling steps that turned to a headlong sprint. Along the way, I fell more than once, scraping my palms and knees upon the ground, but I sprang immediately up again, bounding as a fox from the hunters and hounds, until the sprawl of my home was in sight.

I had just the energy left to throw myself inside, then, directionless and dazed, staggered to the first door I saw to further distance myself from that broken boy outside. After fumbling with the knob, I made it into the dining room, where my legs gave out and the floor rushed up to meet me.

I was vaguely aware that I should get up and go back, lock the door, seek a more secluded area to hide in, but when I braced myself to rise, my limbs only trembled uncontrollably. I didn't know if it was laughter or crying that afflicted me, just that I shook with its effects and could not stop.

It did not matter if I locked every door and shuttered every window.

It did not matter which room I chose.

They could – they would – find me.

Hell had come to Daunderhead, and it had me squarely in its sights.

Chapter Nine

"Henrietta?"

My name echoed faintly, far from the black hole into which I had fallen. Hurried knocks chased it, and the two twirled together, combining and splitting, and braiding again over and around my head, but softly, so softly, hardly bothering me at all.

"Henrietta?"

The raps became sharper and louder, then a distant squeak. Footsteps.

"My God!"

I was jostled, the dark in which I had become cocooned disrupted.

"What's happened to you?"

There was a familiar quality to that voice dancing just outside my grasp. I did not care to chase it. I would have let it go completely, let myself dip back into total unawareness, but the shaking started, and I was no longer free floating, but felt as if I were borne upwards in a sudden rush toward a streak of light.

"Henrietta!"

I flinched as my eyelids peeled apart to a moustached face leaning close over mine.

"You're awake," Mr. Bentley deflated with such relief that rendered him momentarily motionless, then, remembering himself, he placed an arm ever so gingerly around my shoulders and assisted me in sitting up.

"What are you doing here?" I asked, made blunt by the slow dissipating fog that still trapped my thoughts. Flashes of my flight from the cottage, a city, a boy, all crowded together.

"Before he left, your father asked me to come check in on you once or twice, and a good thing too! Where did those bruises come from? Is that blood on your shoes? What happened?" His moustache turned down at its corners. "Did Thorn do this?"

"No," I said, motioning for him to help me up. With his support, I stood and looked around. The dining table and its many chairs took shape, and so too did the full recollection of what led me there. "I must have fainted."

I was sore in ways I'd never experienced, neck inflamed, cheek tender, hands, knees, and legs stinging from what felt like a hundred tiny cuts. Mr. Bentley hovered close at my back as I walked into the hall and looked up and down, from kitchen to entryway. It was so dark, too dark, with all the doors closed and windows covered. I craved light, needed it to chase away the gloom that spread like spilled ink over my heart. A slight limp affected my gait and I bit my lip, feeling again that vice grip around my ankle, which only spurred me more quickly to the front door, left open after Mr. Bentley's arrival, and the sun shining through it.

"You do not need to protect him," Mr. Bentley said gravely. "If he hurt you—"

"It wasn't him. Not really."

"Being a drunkard is not an excuse. His decisions remain his own."

How like Father he sounded.

I half-turned to him, still in the foyer while I blocked the doorway. "You know?"

"Yes," he admitted, and his straightforwardness came as a small surprise. Mr. Bentley had always been more prone to avoiding uncomfortable topics when outside his solicitor's realm, particularly when speaking to a member of the fairer sex. "It has weighed greatly on your father's mind and made him," he paused to search for the

71

most tactful way to complete his thought, "reconsider certain aspects of his estate."

"That's not the whole of it, the drinking." As if my lips had become sewn shut, I found myself unable to provide more. How could I even begin to describe what I'd been through? And how could a man like Mr. Bentley even begin to believe me? He was schooled in facts and logic, relied on them for his livelihood. Even coming from such a dearly held friend's daughter, there was surely no room for demons and curses, for I was starting to think my family *was* cursed, alongside his law books.

"Speak to me, Henrietta," he said, firm and gentle at once. "What else is there?"

I inhaled through my nose, head down, and picked at dirt stuck to my skirt. "Do you believe in the supernatural, Mr. Bentley?"

"I–"

"Because I do," I cut him off before he could offer some insipid answer that would cause me to lose my nerve. "Not just believe, but *know* it exists. And it is terrible."

He observed me through inquisitively narrowed eyes, clearly not having expected me to take such a direction.

As an answer rolled around in his mouth, I added, "Before you speak, know that I am not a widow overtaken with grief. Had it been Victor I'd seen, I would be happily bewitched for the rest of my days. This is something else, a horrible entity that takes many forms and makes me see things. I'm not the only one harassed; Thorn is aware of it too, but it manifests differently for him. In violence. I don't know how it came to settle over Daunderhead, but it has us and will not let go. Thorn knows something, he hinted at it last night, but–"

My heated explanation, only becoming more vehement as I prattled on, was brought to a faltering stop by a puff of white escaping Mr. Bentley. He noticed it too, eyes nearly crossing down his nose, and he exhaled again, emitting another pale cloud despite the mild autumn morning.

Our widened gazes met again as a knock sounded three times in slow, thudding succession from upstairs.

"*Mercy,*" a small voice whispered after the last. "*Please. Mercy.*"

With the stiffness of a man suddenly aware of a predator at his back, Mr. Bentley looked over his shoulder.

Stillness swept over Daunderhead, as if preserving that singular moment of mounting dread. I wasn't sure if the nearly imperceptible shuffling I heard was a product of my overwrought nerves or an actual phenomenon until the petite child appeared at the top of the stairwell. A threadbare cape of grey was hugged around her hunched form, concealing most of her save the hair hanging in damp strings down her back. She lifted one foot high, as if stepping through or over something, and then followed with the other, an exhausted march toward destination unseen.

Had Mr. Bentley not chosen that moment to invoke the Lord's name, perhaps she would have passed us by without ever noticing her audience.

At his voice, she lurched to a halt and shifted her whole body toward us. Ice grew as crystals upon her brows and lashes, freezing her eyes shut, and specks of snow dusted her cape. Shivers ran in twitches through the length of her.

"*Mercy,*" she pleaded through cracked, blackened lips. "*Please. Mercy.*"

The topmost step sighed with her weight. She teetered, buffeted as one might be in heavy wind, and shrank further into her cloak. A tear crept down one white cheek, fast turning to glimmering frost.

"*Mercy.*"

I was the first to regain my senses and grabbed Mr. Bentley by his elbow. My touch roused him from his stupor and together we dove through the door, both scrambling to shut it behind us.

"Do you see?" I asked, gesturing emphatically toward Daunderhead. "I speak the truth!"

The poor solicitor paced in a tight circle, edge of his moustache caught between thumb and forefinger as his lips trembled, unable to form words.

"We are—"

"Haunted," he said, stopping suddenly.

Hearing the word spoken aloud did not alleviate the pit in my stomach. I thought if I could convince him and have him on my side, it would make things easier somehow. But in actuality, it only made me realise how nothing had changed at all. We were still beset with no rhyme or reason by these wraiths.

As I began to spiral into new despair, Mr. Bentley strode past me with significant urgency toward the horse and cart he'd arrived in.

"Come," he said loudly. "We must away at once."

"Where? What about Thorn?"

"If he is inflicted with violent tendencies as you have said, it will be safer for him to stay here."

"Safer?" I repeated indignantly, yet unmoved though he had already mounted the cart's seat. "You've seen what's here with your own eyes. How can you propose we just leave him?"

"Because where we are going is no place for a man who is not in full control of his temper. Now hurry!"

Reluctantly swayed by his ardent display of certainty, I climbed up after him. "What sort of place is this? Where are we going?"

He wrapped the reins once 'round his fists and snapped them over the horse's back. "I know someone who might be able to help."

Mr. Bentley ignored my persistent questions, focusing with great intensity on the horizon ahead. It was tolerable when I had expected our journey to be a short one, turning us toward the village centre, but we passed the crossroad with nary a sideways glance, putting us on a route unfamiliar to me. I had to clutch the cart seat to steady my swaying.

"You've missed the village!" I said, keenly aware he already knew this.

His moustache bristled. "We are not going to the village."

"For goodness sake, I have had it with you men and your obscurity! I have asked you a question, Mr. Bentley, and I damn well expect an answer. A *real* answer."

He started at the rough language I let slip and smacked his lips, acting more like the Mr. Bentley I was so used to, a creature comfortable with predictable roles and rules. I, likewise, had rarely felt much need to wrangle with the demands of my station, which must have made my coarseness that much more shocking to him. That I was not the small girl who used to sit upon his knee, poorly directing his chess plays against Father, was becoming more apparent to both of us, and I wasn't sure I disliked this newer self.

She had seeded, after all, in the arid soils of forbidden love, and fought for every inch of growth, only to have her blooms reaped so low her roots alone were left.

Roots, it would seem, that had again found their purchase.

"Well," Mr. Bentley grumbled, adjusting his glasses, "at least it seems the two of you should get on well."

"Who?"

He sighed and scratched the side of his nose, a clear attempt to delay the inevitable reveal.

"Who?" I repeated more forcefully.

"Alright, alright," he relented. "But first you must promise to withhold any previous opinions you might have formed through rumour and speculation."

I nodded with an uncertain lift of my brow.

"You are familiar, no doubt, with High Hearth?"

"The witch's manor?"

"The same."

I leaned away, studying him with guarded scepticism. Why would he bring up that place? Its very name was enough to invoke the slithering of worms in my belly. No one was stranger to Emmeline Parsings, the lady of the cursed house, or her residence. Hers was a reputation that had been written long before my birth and persisted in whispers. Many names and deeds had been ascribed to her, the Devil's Mistress, suspected of murdering her own husband to strengthen her Hell-drawn magic, and the manor itself had become an occult gate to unimaginable horrors. Sightings of her were rare but always preceded tragedy, and anyone who ventured to High Hearth was likely never to come back, a victim of insatiable bloodthirst and witchcraft.

Though I had never laid eyes on it myself, enough had been said about the manor among the village folk that I could see it clearly, shrouded in low clouds, gargoyle guards on every parapet, dark stone standing against the sea, concealing darker secrets.

"Do not look at me so," he said with a hint of defensiveness. "It is not as people say. I was not at liberty to share my professional association with Mrs. Parsings, but I worked as her solicitor for many years without consequence."

"And now?"

"She passed shortly before your wedding. Upon her death, everything she owned was bequeathed to her next of kin, a great-niece who has since taken ownership of High Hearth."

"I think I remember Mother mentioning that in one of her letters."

"Yes, well, it was quite the to-do for a time," he said with a derisive sniff. "Which is why I did not tell you immediately where we are going. People still have ideas about the family that do not lend themselves to much in the way of courtesy, and the spoiled relationship between the Aldens and the Parsings is no great secret. Had I said I meant to take you to High Hearth, I worried your reaction would be based on bad blood and gossip."

"You still have not said why we are going there," I pointed out, though I could not contest his assumption. "Is this great-niece also a witch? Not," I added quickly, "that I am passing judgement."

A bemused smile touched his features and he considered my question at length.

Finally, he glanced at me and said, "To that I can only attest... she is Eudora."

Chapter Ten

Once we'd put the last of the farmsteads behind us, we travelled down a narrow road through wild country. Trees tinted red and orange with the changing season clustered along hilltops and spread into misted valleys unbroken by man's hand save the single lane we travelled upon. Mr. Bentley warned me it would be a long ride, and I filled it by pestering him for details regarding Eudora Fellowes, but he imparted very little.

"She is an exceedingly private woman," he said when I grew exasperated with his vagueness. "To break her confidence once would be to lose it forever, so I must be mindful of what I say. Details of her time since coming to High Hearth are hers to share. Whatever, if anything, she decides to tell you is entirely up to her."

"But you believe she can help us?"

"I have reason to, yes. I beg you, Henrietta, trust me. I would not bring you all this way if I did not think she would. I will say this for her; hers is a hazelnut's exterior, hard to crack, but I have found it worth the effort. Tillie is especially fond of her and her–"

At mention of his wife, the sweetest soul God had ever placed on His earth, Mr. Bentley winced.

"I forget," he said slowly, conversational tone tinged with hesitancy, "how do you feel about dogs?"

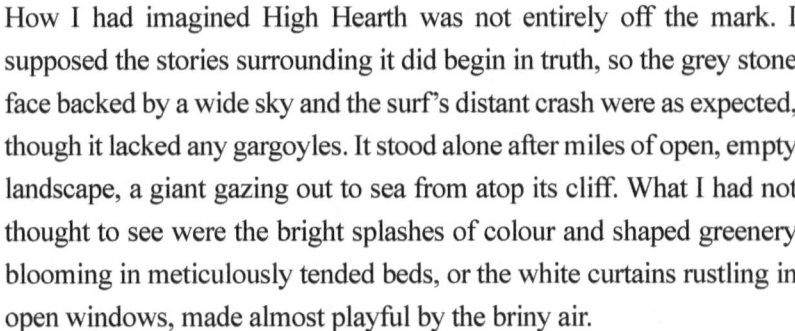

How I had imagined High Hearth was not entirely off the mark. I supposed the stories surrounding it did begin in truth, so the grey stone face backed by a wide sky and the surf's distant crash were as expected, though it lacked any gargoyles. It stood alone after miles of open, empty landscape, a giant gazing out to sea from atop its cliff. What I had not thought to see were the bright splashes of colour and shaped greenery blooming in meticulously tended beds, or the white curtains rustling in open windows, made almost playful by the briny air.

It was as stately a home as I'd ever seen.

"My clothes," I said suddenly, looking down at myself and grabbing a lock of hair hanging freely over my shoulder. I'd been so consumed with the reason for our visit that I had not spared any thought to my bedraggled appearance. "My hair! Mr. Bentley, you cannot present me to Mrs. Fellowes in this way. She will take a single look and wonder what ditch you found me in along the way."

"You need not worry yourself over such things where Eudora is concerned. I will be surprised if she herself is up to your usual standards, especially as we are not expected. In fact, you coming so might work in our favour," he said as he climbed down from the cart.

"Surely not!"

"The haste with which we arrived will tell part of your story by itself. Again, you must trust me on this, my dear."

Even with his reassurances, I dragged my fingers quickly through my hair in attempt to tame it somewhat before accepting his hand to help me down as well.

My feet had hardly touched the ground before the front door swung inward.

I noticed the beasts before the woman. A pair of the hounds so large they seemed more akin to small horses than canines, seated

79

still as statues in the vestibule. Mr. Bentley had said she kept the company of Irish wolfhounds, preferring them over most people, but I had lacked the reference to understand their true scale. They regarded us steadily, giving no indication as to whether or not we were truly welcome. Standing between them in paint-flecked trousers and a man's shirt, with no hint of insecurity in her straight-backed posture, was a woman of middle age, greying hair pulled into a simple chignon at the nape of her neck. She regarded us with the same unreadable coolness as her pets. Their triple gazes did not relent as we approached, and though she and I were nearly of the same height, it felt as if I were stepping into her shadow.

"Hello, Crawford," she said, and finally a warm smile lessened the severity of her features. "I haven't lost track of my days, have I? There's a week yet before our luncheon."

This seemed to have been the cue her dogs were waiting for because they sprang up, tails beating back and forth, and padded to him with tongues lolling. I inched nervously behind the solicitor, who hardly had to bend to give them both a pat upon their blocky heads.

"No, you're quite right with your schedule. I hope we're not interrupting anything," Mr. Bentley said.

"Not at all," she chuckled. "I was just in the middle of my Welsh lesson. Truth be told, the break is a welcome one; it's not one of my better days and the letters have lost all meaning." A subtle change came to her expression then, still a smile, but more reserved, as her attention moved to me. It betrayed nothing of what she made of my physical state. "But who's this?"

"This is Henrietta Ward, daughter of my good friends, Edmund and Leonora Alden."

"It's a pleasure to meet you, Mrs. Fellowes," I said, feeling childish peeking out from behind Mr. Bentley, but it was preferable to keep him between myself and the dogs.

"Eudora, please," she replied, brushing away formalities with a tilt of her head. "You will forgive me for cutting to the point, but what brings you both to High Hearth?"

"Henrietta has found herself in circumstances that I think you are uniquely qualified to assist her with."

"Am I?" Eudora's eyes narrowed shrewdly. "And why might that be?"

"Because my family is haunted," I said, cutting, as she had requested, to the point. "For days now, my cousin and I have been beset by unnatural forces that have only been getting stronger and whose activity has been becoming more frequent."

Had someone come to me and said they were at odds with the occult, I know I would have had some strong reaction; shock, disbelief, questions by the dozen.

But Eudora merely looked me up and down, like I was an insect pinned to a board, and said, "Hmm."

As she studied me, her hounds nosed past Mr. Bentley and began to sniff at my shoes and dress. I kept very still, arms pulled up and clasped across my chest as they circled 'round me, snorting and huffing.

"Black Shuck, Cerberus, to me."

Immediately they, this most suitably named pair, abandoned me to lope back to their owner and retake their seated positions on either side of her. I sighed softly with relief and let my arms drop.

"They're really not so bad once you get used to them," Mr. Bentley said out of the corner of his mouth.

"They're not bad *at all*, Crawford," Eudora corrected him, and it was evident from the way they rolled their eyes at each other this was not the first time they had debated the subject.

"As you say, Eudora."

81

"So can you?" I asked, stepping more fully out from Mr. Bentley's cover to better place myself in the conversation. "Help me, I mean?"

"That depends," Eudora said. "I will need to hear it in detail before I can say one way or the other. You've already made the trip, so you might as well come this way; I'll show you to the drawing room and you may enlighten me."

She snapped her fingers and the dogs trotted inside ahead of us. She began to follow them, and we her, when there came something like a hiss from behind the door. Eudora jerked to a halt and held up a hand, stopping us as well, and turned her head just slightly to look downward, brow knit thoughtfully. When I glanced subtly at Mr. Bentley from beneath my lashes to gauge his impression of such curious behaviour, he was nonplussed, merely cleaning his spectacles with the handkerchief from his breast pocket.

"Nevermind," she said brusquely. "We will instead meet around back in the garden. You know the way along the side of the house; take her, won't you? I'll put the kettle on and meet you out there."

Without giving either of us a chance to question this change, she closed the door firmly behind her and I heard a latch slide into place.

"What was that about?" I asked as I hurried after Mr. Bentley, already strolling toward a flagstone path leading off the drive. "Was someone else in there? I thought you told me she lived alone."

"I can't say," he replied with ambiguity; I did not know if he meant he didn't have an answer, or he simply wouldn't give it to me.

Native flora had been encouraged to grow alongside wide swaths of green lawn around a stone fountain focal point. Mr. Bentley had led me to a white painted gazebo with an open view of the endless ocean behind High Hearth. I sat twisted on the bench seat, chin resting atop my arms on the railing as I watched the waves roll in so far below.

Memories of golden hair floating around an unblinking eye spoiled the view and I turned back around with a shiver.

Eudora arrived with her dogs and a rolling tray of tea and finger sandwiches, the sight of which reminded me how long it had been since my last meal. My eyes must have lingered too obviously on them because she placed a generous portion upon one of the plates and handed it to me before any cups had even been filled. While she served Mr. Bentley and herself, Black Shuck and Cerberus chased each other in a lazy fashion around the gazebo, large paws swiping and stamping. Despite the obvious playful nature of their encounter, the growls that vibrated from their throats made me keep a wary eye on them.

Eudora allowed me the courtesy of finishing my first sandwich before she crossed one leg over the other, tea cup held poised above its saucer, and said, "Whenever you're ready."

"Oh," I mumbled, ducking to wipe crumbs from my lips with an embarrassed blush. "Of course. It's difficult to know where to begin."

"I have found," she said, "that the beginning is a good place."

There were, it turned out, many beginnings that fed into my narrative. The unfortunate circumstances surrounding Thorn's birth, how he had come to live in Daunderhead, the marriage that had taken me from it, our separate returns, and everything that had happened since. I wept in my recount of Victor and again detailing Thorn's most recent behaviours, a hand pressed over the cheek he'd struck. At my tears, the hounds, who had been lying at Eudora's feet, whined softly, nudging towards me with lowered heads and low wagging tails. I let them near with some trepidation, stroking them with only the very tips of my fingers, but the calm with which they settled beside me had a spreading effect, and I was soon petting them properly, soothed by the feel of their warm, wiry coats.

Mr. Bentley added what little he could from what Father had told him of Thorn and what had prompted him to bring me there after discovering me on the floor.

"It was a ghost, I am sure of it," he said, and I looked up from Cerberus' head, resting in my lap.

"A ghost? No, it couldn't be, there are no spirits in Daunderhead. I would know. It must be something else, the result of a curse placed upon my family or hellish conjuring."

"Places are not the only things that can be haunted," Eudora explained. "Anything that a person had an especially strong attachment to in life can become their anchor after death. Sometimes, they're not even the ones still holding on."

"What do you mean?"

But she shifted her attention back to Mr. Bentley. "What did you see, Crawford?"

"A little girl, perhaps seven or eight, dressed as a pauper. Her presence affected the environment to some degree, making visible my breath, though not so strong as to lower the actual temperature. She knocked on a door, begging for mercy, and then did the same when she came upon us. Judging by that and her look, she froze whilst seeking shelter."

"So she would've been frightened," Eudora said.

"Undoubtedly."

"But how would an unfortunate child have become attached to the Aldens or their home?" she mused, lips pursed. "Does anyone in your family work with children, Henrietta?"

I shook my head.

"What of the others you've seen? You mentioned a woman in your bathtub?"

"Yes, she tried to drown me."

"Do you remember anything specific about her?"

"Her eye, mostly. She was staring up at me with such terror. And once, when I got my head above the water, it was as if I were at sea instead of in a bathroom. It only lasted for a second, but it was so real I could still smell it even after she vanished again."

"More fear," Eudora nodded slightly. "You didn't feel any animosity from her?"

"No. I only felt afraid."

"Hmm. Go on, what else?"

"There was a burned person in Thorn's cottage and a bludgeoned boy on the lane between it and Daunderhead. He, the boy, grabbed my ankle and suddenly I was in a city the same way I'd been in the ocean with the woman. I'm sorry I can't explain it any more clearly than that."

"You're doing fine," she assured me. "In most cases, ghosts are as much memory as they are actual *things*. They're made up of powerful emotions, commonly a particularly potent one captured at the moment they died. Imagine how you would feel if you were burning or beaten to the point of death: frightened, alone, desperate for someone to come to your aid. If that desperation were intense enough, it could trap the soul, keeping it in those last, traumatic moments. When particularly agitated, their reality can bleed into ours, giving us such glimpses as you've described. The primary question remains how they came to be at your home, which is near neither sea nor city."

"What of Thorn?" I leaned forward, disturbing Cerberus, who withdrew with a huff. "If it's ghosts as you say, then why is he driven to fits of rage?"

Eudora and Mr. Bentley traded a look not lost to me.

"I am not so naive to think his drinking is not a problem or that it does not affect him," I said sharply. "This is something different! It's like he becomes someone else; I hardly recognize him."

85

"That's not unheard of with lushes, Henrietta," Mr. Bentley replied gently.

I balled my hands upon my lap and stared sullenly over the water again, biting the inside of my cheek to keep from snapping further. Mr. Bentley straightened his coat lapels and cleared his throat with some discomfort, but I could feel Eudora observing me with cool repose over the top of her cup.

I made myself meet her gaze with a defiant lift of my chin. "The words he uses are not his own. We grew up in the same house, had the same tutors, read the same books; he never referred to women as 'tarts' or said things like 'ain't' before."

"You don't think his time as a bobby would introduce such colloquialisms?"

"Coroner's officer," I corrected her. Thorn had been promoted off the street early in his career, something we'd all been very proud of. "But no, not as he used them that night."

Thinking of how he'd spoken to me, so callously, triggered another memory, one so uncertain I debated not mentioning it, but ultimately decided it was better for Eudora to have all the information I could offer, no matter how absurd it sounded.

"Twice I have encountered this other self, and both times, there has been some sort of…glint or glimmer that passes over him. Like a sheer veil that vanishes completely after it falls into place. Could that mean something?"

Eudora's finger had begun to tap against the side of her saucer and she lowered it, setting her cup down atop it. "Perhaps," she conceded hesitantly. "But if what I'm now thinking is correct, it's not something I've encountered before outside my books, and even then I've not read deeply into the matter. I would need to do additional research."

"Whatever you need to do, we can wait! Maybe help, even. Where are your books? I'm quite a good reader—"

"No," she stopped short my enthusiastic offer. "Thank you."

"Why? We're already here." I looked imploringly to Mr. Bentley, but he only shrugged.

"I cannot allow you into High Hearth, Henrietta. Yours is a fragile soul currently rife with grief, making you particularly sensitive to the supernatural. You are like a beacon, and your heightened emotion feeds theirs, which makes them stronger. It's why the ghosts of Daunderhead keep finding you."

"That shouldn't matter; they can't have followed all the way here, can they?"

Eudora smiled thinly as she stood. "It's not your ghosts I'm worried about. Take the rest of the sandwiches for the road if you like. I will call upon you tomorrow at your residence after I've confirmed my suspicions."

"Thank you, Eudora," Mr. Bentley said and offered an arm to help me up, but I was not so satisfied and rose without aid.

"What *are* your suspicions, exactly?" I asked, setting my hands on my hips.

She eyed me pensively, then said, "Some ghosts are not trapped, per se. They are not born of sudden bursts during final breaths. They are formed from hard lives, and the rage formed with them is what keeps them in our world. These are the dangerous ones, who seek to punish and spread their pain. You would do well to stay away from your cousin, Henrietta."

"Why?"

"Because I have reason to believe one such ghost is attempting to possess him."

Chapter Eleven

Black Shuck and Cerberus ran alongside the cart until we turned out of the drive, at which point Mr. Bentley commanded them to return to Eudora, who stood waiting in front of High Hearth. As the manor and its inhabitants gradually shrank behind us, I furrowed my brow and turned to Mr. Bentley.

"We came all this way for such a brief meeting?"

"A valuable one nonetheless. She is not overly fond of most, but you could not ask for a more steadfast companion, especially in a situation like this. Having her on our side will certainly tip the scales."

I gave a backwards glance while I considered the enigmatic woman. "What did she mean when she said it wasn't my ghosts she was worried about?"

But he only pushed his spectacles up his nose with a short, dry cough. "I can't say."

I had much to dwell on during our two hour return trip. That I was somehow acting as a beacon to these ghosts, calling them forth with my sorrow, made it so much harder to bear. Grieving was made difficult enough with the living, however well intentioned they might be, but now I had the added burden of the responsive dead?

Fate continued to deal from an unjust deck.

Whatever part my sensitivities played in the greater picture, however, it did not explain how the spirits had come to infect my ancestral home. As Eudora so astutely pointed out, Daunderhead was far from any ocean or cityscapes as shown to me, making it evident they had not died upon the property and laid dormant until I roused them, and I had no connection to any of the apparitions that I was aware of. It seemed equally unlikely that they all shared an attachment to the same item and came part and parcel with some antique Mother had unwittingly purchased.

Which left only one other option.

"Coroner's officers investigate suspicious deaths, don't they?" I mumbled more to myself than Mr. Bentley, but he heard and took the inquiry as meant for him.

"They determine if there's a suitable reason for an inquest, which is usually necessary if a cause of death is sudden or uncertain, yes."

Drowning. Burning. Bludgeoned. Freezing. Those certainly sounded like they'd fall under Thorn's jurisdiction.

"They'd examine the bodies closely then? Learn about the victims?"

"Correct."

I was blind to the scenic mid-afternoon rolling past, seeing only Thorn, still a new father, crouched over a small girl with crystal lashes lying in the snow.

"How would it feel, Mr. Bentley?" I turned to him. "Day after day, faced with naught but death. And the worst sort at that, driven by cruelty and neglect. The seamy side of society, not only exposed but sliced open for you to gaze into, dirty your hands in. What might that do to a man?"

Catching on, he rubbed his thumb introspectively along his chin. "It's enough to drive him to drink."

"Especially if it followed him home."

"But it's my understanding ghosts need some sort of significant link to a person in order to remain with them. Thorn most likely wouldn't have had any real relationship with the subjects of his investigations."

89

"No," I agreed, head bobbing as I rapidly rearranged my thoughts. "Not while they were alive, anyway. Eudora said it's not necessarily the ghosts who are the ones holding on."

"You think…"

"Thorn has always had a gentle heart. The trauma of their deaths probably created the spirits, but he's the one who witnessed their end and would think about them day after day, what they must have gone through, be left with images of their faces. Maybe there were some he just could not put behind him. Maybe there are some he carries still."

"Thus creating the necessary link."

Mr. Bentley and I shared a troubled look that revealed we'd come to the same conclusion.

If I were a beacon, feeding them with my grief, Thorn was the wellspring from which they flowed.

Had there ever been such a self-absorbed creature as I?

Thorn had known, had practically told me as much, but I, so consumed with casting myself as damsel in distress, hadn't listened.

Pay it no heed. For your own good, let it lie. Go home.

Do not come back here.

He had known, and he'd wanted to protect me from it, determined to face his ghosts alone, something I would never allow.

When Mr. Bentley began to slow the cart in front of Daunderhead, I compelled him to continue on and take us instead to the cottages. He was not without his reservations, however, and reined the horse to a halt.

"We should wait to confront him," he advised. "Eudora told you to stay away from him for a reason. Let her do her research so we're better prepared."

"I am so grateful to you, Mr. Bentley," I said, earnestly grasping his forearm. "Please do not think I'm not. But if you do not move this cart down that path, I will push you out of it and do it myself."

He blinked twice, eyes owlishly wide, and sputtered, but we began moving again.

"At least when Eudora and I were at odds over where we were going, she only threatened to get down herself and walk," he grumbled from beneath his moustache.

On the way to the cottage, I pointed out the spot where I'd encountered the injured boy and delved into greater detail about what he looked like and the street we'd been on while he maintained physical contact.

"Did he try to hurt you?" Mr. Bentley asked.

I considered his question carefully through the lens of fresh perspective. "No, I don't think so. He held me by the ankle, but never painfully, and he made no attempt that I noticed to harm me."

"So it's possible he's benign like the waif seemed to be."

"I think they all might be."

"But the woman in the tub tried to drown you."

"I'm not so sure," I said. "Eudora asked if I felt animosity from her, but I didn't. I thought the fear that I *did* feel was all mine, but perhaps I was wrong. Maybe she was just afraid, looking for something to hold on to, and I happened to be there. She wasn't trying to hurt me; she was trying to save herself. Thinking on them all now, I don't think I got a sense of malice from any of them."

"Except Thorn."

"The one possessing him, not Thorn himself."

"Right," he tipped his head in acquiescence. "But how do we know that one isn't one you've already encountered?"

"We don't, but my cousin likely does."

Once we arrived at the cottage, I did not wait for Mr. Bentley to come to a complete stop before hopping down from the seat and running toward the open door.

"Henrietta!"

Ignoring him, I went in, lips parted to shout for Thorn, but the crunch of glass under my boots silenced me. The main room looked as if a whirlwind had swept through, knocking all its furniture askew and smashing the bottles I'd left on the desk upon the floor.

"Oh dear," Mr. Bentley uttered softly as he came to stand behind me.

"Thorn?" I yelled, darting to the kitchen, which had received similar treatment to the previous room, and was similarly empty.

The steps creaked as the solicitor ascended to the first floor, likewise calling out.

After a brief look out the back, I returned to the main room, where I met Mr. Bentley.

"He's not upstairs," he said. "Could he have gone searching for work?"

"I don't think so. Look at this place; he was in no right mind to go job seeking."

His expression grew serious as his eyes swept over the upturned sofa and shards of glass. "He could've gone looking for you in Daunderhead. Not as Thorn, but as the other. He might be waiting there still."

The implication made me shudder and I wrapped my arms around myself. "Then we should go there next," I said in spite of my skipping heart.

"It would be safer if I went alone. I can bring you to mine first, Tillie would welcome your company."

"No. Thorn needs to know he's not alone in this. His family is with him, always."

At his instance, Mr. Bentley took the lead into Daunderhead. We cleared each room together, going from parlour to Father's office, to the dining and drawing rooms. As much as I wanted to believe there was no reason to fear Thorn, I walked on tiptoe behind Mr. Bentley, checking frequently over my shoulder to ensure we weren't being followed.

"The billiard room door is open," Mr. Bentley pointed out, keeping his voice low. "Did you leave it so?"

"I don't remember."

A shaft of afternoon light illuminated the hall from within as if inviting us to enter. We huddled just outside its glow, straining to hear any subtle sounds of a person lying in wait.

But what we heard was a reverberating snore rip through the air.

Thorn was sitting upright against the far wall beside the liquor cabinet, his legs sprawled in front of him and head drooped against his chest. A boozy miasma hovered around him, a product of the nearly empty bottle of amber liquid on its side next to him.

Mr. Bentley and I walked slowly around the billiard table, wary that it might be some trick, but Thorn only continued his raucous snoring without stirring.

I sighed, frustration and compassion turning as two sides of the same coin as we stood over my oblivious cousin. "Even if we were able to wake him, he'd not be coherent enough to confirm any of our guesswork regarding the ghosts."

"I'm afraid you're right. We can come back tomorrow and wait for Eudora—"

"I thought I made it clear I will not be leaving him."

"He is dangerous in ways we are not equipped to handle."

"He's unconscious!"

"For now."

It was difficult to argue when we both knew how right he was. I chewed my lower lip, gaze flicking between Mr. Bentley's sympathetic frown and Thorn. I only needed to come up with a way to guarantee our safety, then Mr. Bentley could not take issue with our staying.

"There's rope in the stable," I said, perking up with an idea. "I'll fetch it and we'll bind him. He won't be a risk to us then."

"Henrietta…"

I took his hand between mine and squeezed it with a frail smile. "I will not beg you to stay, Mr. Bentley; go if you wish. I understand, Thorn would too. But I cannot. He has woken up to only empty bottles too often already."

I turned and hurried away, still intent on getting my rope.

But, despite my show of bravado, I deeply hoped Mr. Bentley would be there when I returned.

He had removed his coat and was sitting in an armchair in front of the unlit fireplace when I returned with a coil of rope pulled over one shoulder.

"You stayed," I said, unashamed of the grin that accompanied the words.

"Yes, well," he made a small, slightly awkward gesture, as if to brush aside any oncoming emotive gratitude, and crossed to me, taking the rope. "You understand it could be hours before he wakes."

"I know."

I followed him over to Thorn and observed as he wrapped two, tight loops around his wrists, ran a length down his legs, and repeated the process at his ankles before tying it off in a heavy knot.

"Is it enough?" I asked, my question held together by anxious threads.

94

"For the physical body, it should be. What haunts him is another matter. I'm not so learned in this area, but I do know we'd be wise to lay salt across the threshold. They cannot cross it."

After retrieving the salt box from its hook in the kitchen, I spread a white line across the billiard room doorway, then we took the extra precaution of pouring a thick circle around Thorn, using up almost our entire supply.

"Be careful not to disturb it," Mr. Bentley warned. "It must remain unbroken to be effective."

So gravely was this advice given that I knotted off the end of my skirt to prevent it from dragging across the ground.

We came and went as little as possible in the ensuing hours, leaving only to stable Mr. Bentley's horse and prepare a simple supper of cold ham slices, pickled onions, and cheese, for I could not find it in me to cook a meal I hardly felt like eating in the first place. As dusk pushed back the daylight, Mr. Bentley lit a fire in the hearth, and we sat much as we had in the carriage after he'd found me at the station, him providing enough of the conversation for the both of us to fill the silence that grew in the dark of Daunderhead Hall.

I could only watch my cousin, and wait for him to wake.

Chapter Twelve

Even Mr. Bentley could only carry on for so long before becoming tired of the sound of his own voice, and once he trailed off, all that was left to ward off the creeping night was the fire's crackle. We took turns keeping it fed, stoking it, making sure we didn't lose our light as the world turned to black outside the windows. At one point, the solicitor helped himself to a tipple of port, poured with a slight tremble, and nursed it while staring at his reflection in a glass pane.

The clock ticked loudly from the mantle, announcing each second as if to mock us with how slowly they seemed to pass.

Restlessness grew as the hours did. After sitting so long in a single spot, I left the chair and skimmed the titles filling the built-in bookshelves on either side of the fireplace. Though not quite in line with the more frivolous tastes I'd developed since widowhood, there were plenty of hardbound copies of Greek classics, essays, and historical accounts to choose from. I selected a few and made an honest attempt at engagement, but the pages might as well have been blank for all the meaning they held for me. Alternatively, Mr. Bentley seemed content enough when he relieved me of one of the hefty tomes and sat reading with his spectacles perched at the end of his nose.

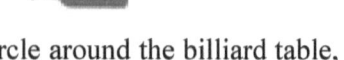

I was walking in an idle circle around the billiard table, rolling one of the ivory balls along its perimeter, when a log gave way with a jarring snap, eaten through by fire. Already on edge, I jumped and glared at the offending hearth, eliciting a weak chuckle from Mr. Bentley. The flames leapt around their kindling, embers drifting up the flue, and another log shifted.

Fingers, skin charred and cracked, stretched from underneath it.

The ball slipped from my grasp and landed with a clatter on the floor before rolling away to knock against the bottom of Thorn's boot. The noise of it drew a wince from my cousin, noticed out of the corner of my eye, and his head rolled to one side, but my gaze was frozen on the arms slithering out from between the burning wood. They flailed, pawing at the grating, using it to pull their head, hairless, all scorched and split with red, maw wrenched wide, free. The fire roared around it, licking the hearth's edges and billowing heat into the room. The reek of burning hair and bubbling flesh rolled with it.

The burned figure's mouth contorted with a rasping cry.

All at once, Mr. Bentley had me by the shoulders and was pulling me back, putting distance between myself and the fiery ghost.

"Stay back! It might not intend to hurt us, but so caught in its torment, it may not even realise the danger it presents."

"The salt," I said, taking hold of his shirt sleeve. "I thought they couldn't cross it!"

"They can't." He manoeuvred me behind him, continuing to back away until the billiard table was between us and the fireplace.

"Then how—" The end of the question lodged like an ice chip in my throat.

It did not have to cross the salt. It wasn't coming from elsewhere in the house.

Lacking forethought in our haste, we had confined it to the same room as its source.

The floor sizzled beneath its palms as it extracted its torso from the logs.

"No," Thorn slurred woefully, picking his head up. "No, no, no."

His eyes swam back and forth, trying to make sense of the scene unfolding before him.

"*Mercy.*"

My scream appeared as a translucent mist when the small girl whispered at our backs. She reached out, pale hands tipped with the black mark of frostbite, but we staggered beyond her grasp. Her blue lips quivered and streaks of crystal shimmered down her cheeks.

"*Please.*"

"No," Thorn repeated, tears welling. "I wish to sleep...I just want to sleep."

From beneath the billiard table, splayed on his stomach, a red-stained face gazed up at us. He opened his mouth like he too meant to speak, to give voice to the desperate need that burned in his eyes, but only blood and teeth spilled forth. He clutched his broken skull with a wet, choked sob.

"I'm sorry," Thorn moaned.

A silhouette filled the open doorway across from us. Water dripped in steady cadence from her dangling feet, suspended inches off the floor. Her golden hair flowed around her, a halo outlined in the red glow of fire. She thrashed, kicking and writhing, hands clawing at the air. Her eye swivelled wildly back and forth in its socket.

Mr. Bentley and I pressed into the corner, clinging to one another as the ghosts limped and pulled themselves toward us. My breathing turned to shallow gasps clogged by smoke and iron and rot. Their cacophony of suffering surrounded us like a storm from which it seemed there would be no end.

But at the sight of Thorn's shoulders shaking, my heart constricted, breaking at the anguish stroked in harsh lines across his face. Not even as a child had I ever seen pain etched so baldly upon him. And he was so much a boy then, one who had forgotten the taste of hope, afraid, so lost and tumbling further.

I had to catch him.

Though terror had its fangs in me, I sidled away from Mr. Bentley, body kept tight to window and wall, face turned as far from the ghosts as possible, and I knelt beside Thorn, keeping the line of salt between us.

"Netta," he wept, hardly able to focus on me. "I want to sleep."

"You can't. We need your help."

"I can't."

"Thorn, please. How do we get rid of them? How can we help you?"

"I can't!"

"Talk to me!"

"Henrietta!"

I spun at Mr. Bentley's shout, expecting to see him encircled, only to find him standing alone, hands still upheld to hold off a threat that was no longer there.

"They're gone," he said, as if not quite convinced it were true.

My heart beat loud as an orchestra drum in my ears as I straightened. The fire had dwindled back down to its norm, no longer a blaze reaching beyond its bed. A puddle remained where the drowned woman had been and a series of handprints burned into the wood led from the hearth, but the ghosts themselves had indeed vanished.

I took no relief in it, though.

The hairs rose along the back of my neck. Something had changed, so subtle I'd not yet consciously perceived it but recognized it nonetheless. It wriggled beneath my skin, becoming an unsettling itch that made me want to crawl out of my own body. I scanned the room nervously, overwhelmed by that sense of wrongness.

There was nothing amiss in the books or the chairs or the table.

It was the shadows.

Gathered in the corner beside the fireplace, diagonal to our own position, they lay with a blanket's thickness, so dark I realised I couldn't make out the painting hung there. A chill travelled from the tips of my toes up my legs, and I reflexively took a step back, swallowing hard.

"There," I whispered, gesturing limply.

This was not like the others, who had instilled fright and sparked in me the desire to run. There was no desire to run now. It was a *need*, deeply ingrained and animalistic, that howled for me to flee.

But the dark rolled forward.

I was thrown from Thorn and slammed into the billiard table. The edge caught me just under my ribs, forcing the air from my lungs, and my face was dragged against the baize as a hand closed in my hair. It ripped my head back and brought it down against the table, creating an explosion of stars behind my closed lids. Ringing filled my ears, muffling shouts from behind. I was yanked up once more and managed to brace my arms against the table, keeping myself from being viciously knocked a second time. I was rewarded with what felt like a sledgehammer swinging into my side.

Through agonised tears, I saw Mr. Bentley run by, long strides carrying him to the door. He stooped, swept his hand across the floor, and spun in a single move, casting a trail of powdery white across the air.

The shadow vanished from around me with a snarl that shook the windows as the salt rained down and I dropped to my knees, hands clasped around my throbbing middle.

"Netta," Thorn groaned and, as if ignorant of the rope binding him, tried unsuccessfully to find his feet. He slid back down the wall, in doing so nudging the ball I'd dropped earlier and sending it rolling back to me.

"Are you alright?" Mr. Bentley asked.

His panicked query ended in a shout as he was hoisted upward in a swirl of black, the collar of his shirt twisted at his neck. He kicked frantically, hands groping uselessly at his throat against his assailant's hold. He sailed, screaming, into a bookshelf and fell hard at its base, where the shadow again set upon him, hurling him across the floor into the chairs.

The certainty that it would not stop until it killed him knelled like clashing bells within me and I spun on my knees, looking for some way to stop it. The salt had just made it angrier, only driving it away until the granules landed in a broken spread that it went around to attack Mr. Bentley. I tore at my hair, wracked with dry, breathless sobs, helplessness closing like a noose.

And I did what I had always done.

I turned to my big brother.

Slack jawed and glassy eyed, he shook his head in a wide, sluggish arc. "Sleep," he murmured to himself, trying to deny Mr. Bentley's weakening cries. "I just need…"

I wanted to scream. I would have, had I been able to force my voice out. Love and loathing had never lived so closely in my heart and they combined into such a passionate rage.

Sleep? That fury bellowed, *All you do is sleep! Where have you been when I needed you most but drowned in ale?*

When I went to him after the woman in the tub. When first I encountered the burned figure. Now.

Where was Thorn?

Awake, I realised with a lightning's jolt.

The night I'd confronted him, drunk myself, but him sober, when first I'd seen the silhouettes at his back. And when I'd gone to him the next morning after the ghost had disappeared so suddenly from the bath, the alcohol had still been fresh on his breath. He couldn't

101

have been unconscious for long. And again, the burned figure in the rocking chair; it had only appeared when his breathing had changed. When he'd started to rouse.

How quiet had our evening been until he'd awoken?

Sleep, he'd said.

He only needed to sleep.

The crash of Mr. Bentley's body against a wall snatched me from my thoughts and I looked around with renewed fervour. My fingers brushed the solid, ivory billiard ball. I did not have time to consider my options. To think would be to lose what little courage I had. Mr. Bentley could not afford it.

I grabbed it, arm already cocking back as I jumped up and lurched toward Thorn.

His eyes were half closed, lips moving soundlessly in silent plea for sleep. His, our, escape. I raised the ball higher, teeth clenched, chest heaving.

He tilted his head back. There was no questioning in his expression, no understanding of what I meant to do. Only pain.

"I'm sorry, Thorn," I whispered.

I wailed as the ball connected with the side of his head. He teetered, exhaling in disbelief, and the shadow over Mr. Bentley's prone body flickered. Its attack upon the solicitor ceased at once, and I felt its white hot hatred turn toward me.

A roar filled Daunderhead as I brought the ball down on my cousin's head again, and then, only silence.

Until I began to scream.

Chapter Thirteen

I pressed both hands over my mouth to stifle my despair and stared at Thorn, fearing for a long moment I had struck too hard in the wrong place. It was only when I was certain he was still breathing that I could pry myself from his side and go to Mr. Bentley, left lying in a pile of books that had fallen from their shelves. Swelling had already begun to close one eye and his lip was split, bloodying his moustache. It was immediately clear his face would be a mask of bruises come the next day. His left arm was bent beneath him, and from its angle, I could only guess it was broken.

He expelled a ragged grunt as I removed a book laying flat across his stomach, a sound sweeter than any angel's song.

"Lie still," I instructed, worried if he moved some yet undiscovered injury would worsen itself. "I don't know how badly hurt you are."

"Very," he said. "But not enough to kill me."

The smile he tried to force for my benefit was short lived, turning to a tight grimace, and I reflexively reached out, wanting to soothe him, but not knowing where or how to begin, so my hands merely hung ineffectually over him.

"There's a decanter on the top shelf of the cabinet, in the very middle," he said, mouth hardly moving. "Get it for me."

I hurried to do as he asked, fetching the requested item. I thought he might pour the liquor over some of the wounds seeping through his shirt, but instead, he instructed me to remove the topper and sat up enough to take a long drink.

"It will dull the pain for the time being."

Eager for any sort of task that would render me useful, I quickly offered, "I can bring you laudanum. I'm sure we have some."

"No, I don't tolerate the stuff," he said. "I want to keep more of my wits than it would allow." Although suffering was writ in his every movement, his hand still found mine. "Are you alright? And Thorn?"

"I think so. But I had to…" Tears burned in my eyes and I looked at the man slouched in a ring of salt. "The ghosts coordinate with his consciousness. When I understood that, I-I had to stop it. I didn't want to hurt him."

"He knows that," Mr. Bentley assured me, words clipped by a tremor of pain.

"What can I do?" I begged, too afraid to touch him.

"One more drink. Then, we will see about getting me off this floor."

It was an undertaking easier said than done, and by the time we managed to get Mr. Bentley seated in one of the armchairs, we were both near to tears. At the slightest twinge of his arm, he shrieked, and any pressure upon his torso evoked a sharp gasp, leading him to believe his ribs had not made it through the altercation intact. Again I offered laudanum without success.

"Tea," he said weakly, beads of sweat dotting his hairline. "And hot towels, if you don't mind."

I certainly did not and played nurse to his every whim. Soon he had steaming towels laid across his shoulder, head, and chest, a quilt across his legs, feet propped up, with a tray of tea and a small selection of food within reach of his working arm. My own aches seemed paltry in comparison and, when not ensuring he had every comfort I could provide him, I was sitting near to Thorn, both to observe him for signs of waking and to convince myself he was still alive.

I dozed at points, though never long, and never fully. Every time I began to descend into deeper sleep, my body would jerk awake with a rush of panic, positive that something was stalking the room from the shadows.

But each time, it was a fear unfounded. Thorn remained unresponsive, and so too did his ghosts.

I passed into morning this way, stealing seconds of rest between tending to the solicitor and monitoring my cousin. Mr. Bentley only grew more uncomfortable, every twinge and shift a new pain. When I again pressed the issue of medication, he staunchly refused with nails dug into the arms of his chair.

"No. If they return—"

"You will be in no condition to do anything if there's anything that can be done at all." As far as I could tell, there was only one way to put an end to their activity, and it was not one Mr. Bentley would be capable of carrying out, nor one I relished having to repeat.

"No," was all he said again, waxy features carved into a determined countenance.

In his stubbornness, initially vexing, I began to recognize the same aspects that had caused me to insist on staying with Thorn despite the danger. The unwillingness to leave the other alone. The desire to protect. The love. Mr. Bentley could no more abandon me to an intoxicated sleep than he could when he still had the ability to walk away.

And I realised more than ever how blessed I had always been to have a second father in Crawford Bentley.

"Then I will take a horse and bring the doctor and Mrs. Bentley. She must be sick with worry."

"No time; Eudora is likely already on her way."

"It's still so early."

A wry light entered his pale eyes, squinted against his maladies. "Time holds little meaning when you're facing such an urgent matter as putting a social obligation behind you."

At his persuasion, I went to my room, changed into clean clothing, and plaited my hair, pinning it tight to my scalp. Wearing it loose had made it a target to be used against me, a mistake I would not make again.

To better clear my mind, I brewed a strong black coffee paired with a hearty breakfast of eggs, sausage, and tomato. Mr. Bentley ate sparingly, preferring the softer foods, while I cleared my plate with ravenous enthusiasm and still had the appetite to accept whatever he didn't finish. I was scraping the last bits from my plate when a heavy knock sounded upon Daunderhead's front door.

Mr. Bentley's moustache turned up just slightly in a weary, expectant smile. "Ah," he said. "The cavalry."

Eudora Fellowes, adorned in a cycling costume with bloomers and a short jacket, greeted me with a curt nod. A leather satchel, made weighty by its contents, hung against her hip, and her loyal hounds flanked her to either side.

At any other time, I might have found her attire odd, even scandalous, but right then she could have appeared in the nude and it would have been welcome.

"There's been an incident," I said immediately, dispensing with any greeting, and invited her to follow. Black Shuck and Cerberus padded in behind her, noses pressed to the floor with intense interest.

"What's happened?" she asked as we walked to the billiard room, and I provided a quick summary to prepare her for what lay ahead. Even with such knowledge, she gasped upon seeing Mr. Bentley and, after commanding her dogs to sit, hurried to his side.

"You fools; I told you to stay away from him," she said harshly, though her touch upon his arm was tender.

"She listens as well as you," he said.

"Do not waste your energy speaking, especially if it is to mock my concern," she replied, lines on her face deepening as she fought a poignant smile.

"It's my fault. I couldn't," I began to explain, but my voice cracked.

"It's no one's fault, my dear."

"What's done is done," Eudora said firmly. "You're both still alive, which is a better start than the alternative. Now we must focus on what comes next."

I wiped my eyes with a hurried sniff. "You found something?"

"I believe so," she said, looking to Thorn. The combination of booze and billiard ball continued to hold, but we were all aware our time was borrowed. "But it will require his willing participation."

"Impossible," I said. "Once he wakes, so will they. They're—"

"Connected to him, yes. I figured that much out after you left."

"How?"

"Simple mathematics. The house itself was not haunted, nor were you, as evidenced by the fact nothing accompanied you to High Hearth. With no one else in residence at the present time, it fell to reason that your cousin was the only one left to whom they might be tethered. More precisely, his energy. All ghosts require it to assume a substantial form. In places, it soaks into the foundation and, while a steadier supply, keeps them imprisoned at that singular location. It would seem people provide that energy in spurts when they're particularly agitated and their emotions are running high. It means they can't be as active, but they will go where their person goes, and more powerful entities will consume more energy, driving lesser ones away. Combine his moods with yours, and you both create quite the potent cocktail from which the spirits draw."

All my confrontations, meant with the best intentions to help Thorn find his way back to himself, had unwittingly pitched him further into his darkness. A hand drifted to my lips, parted in contrite shock.

107

"I was making it worse," I murmured. "I shouted at him, demanded he tell me why he'd become this way. He didn't want to, but I pushed and pushed."

"You couldn't have known, Henrietta," Mr. Bentley said.

"No, and I doubt he did either. All he probably knew was that being drunk made it so he didn't see them. And therein lies our problem." Eudora folded her arms over her chest with a sigh. "Rather than face his ghosts, he bottles them away and makes strangers of his loved ones, unwittingly doing the very things making him most vulnerable to possession. Loneliness and hopelessness make cracks in the soul that evil is eager to fill. For this to work, Thorn must confront what's tying the spirits to him."

"Then we'll tell him that. Once he knows what must be done–"

"If only it were so simple. You approach this as a woman, someone allowed, even encouraged, to display a range of emotions. Setting aside all the backwards tedium that accompanies being labelled the more sensitive sex, there is a certain degree of benefit to be derived from it. Alternatively, men are expected to get by with thick skin and bootstraps. They are faulted creatures, but it is society as a whole we have to thank for their poor introspective abilities."

Without moving at all, Eudora slapped me soundly across the face, revealing my jaundiced eye. Had I not stood before Thorn and insisted he be more a man? What had I truly been asking of him while he was already laid so low? Take ownership, responsibility, make right this situation I don't fully fathom but have laid squarely upon your shoulders. I had done as my father before me, belittling the essence of his being for perceived weakness whilst hardly trying to understand how we had reached that point.

In the same breath, I'd asked him to share his pain with me and then told him he had no right to it and needed only to find a solution.

I had to rectify it.

"What do we do?" I asked softly.

"We need to get him to more neutral ground to avoid tainting the house with residual activity. The deep ties to the estate and the energy that already exists here would be ripe for creating new bonds. I already have the location selected: the cemetery."

Mr. Bentley and I baulked at her suggestion.

"A cemetery?" he said. "You can't be serious. Do you mean to stir every ghost in the village?"

"On the contrary, hallowed grounds are some of the least supernaturally inclined. They are places of Godly rest, which repel the restless, and people rarely form the necessary attachment to them to beget a haunting. They are not like homes or places of work, where we spend our lives, and so they are not where we spend our earth bound deaths. It is a safe and quiet place in which to draw out Thorn's spirits, where they will be unlikely to linger should we succeed."

"Are you sure it would not be wiser to do it elsewhere?"

"We'll do it there," I said, squaring my shoulders. "If you say it is our best option, Eudora, I will trust you."

She inclined her head toward me with a brow lifted in brief triumph at Mr. Bentley. "Thank you. But now that I've seen the size of him and we are down Crawford's assistance, I must ask: how are we getting him there?"

Chapter Fourteen

It was not easy to get Thorn out of Daunderhead. After Mr. Bentley suggested the use of his horse and cart, Eudora and I took my cousin each by a bound ankle and hauled him through the halls. Our jostling drew sighs and grunts from Thorn, though he still trailed limply behind us with eyes shut, and it was cause enough to redouble our efforts.

Like dark spectres themselves, Black Shuck and Cerberus came after us, but theirs was not the relaxed lope I'd witnessed before. After each sniffing Thorn as we pulled him past, they'd shaken their heads, ears pulled back, and fallen in line behind us with eyes only for him.

"They won't hurt him, will they?" I asked nervously as we went 'round a corner, Thorn's shoulder knocking against a floorboard.

"No," Eudora said. "They're sensitive to spiritual activity and must be aware something's amiss in Thorn. Don't worry about them."

But with their lowered gazes locked so tenaciously, I found it a difficult request.

Once we'd manoeuvred Thorn out of the house beneath an overcast sky, Eudora shed her satchel and ordered her hounds to stand guard over him, furthering my uneasiness. But there was no opportunity for prolonged fretting as she directed me to lead her to the stable. Together we hitched horse to cart and rode it to the front of the house, where I was relieved to see Thorn still lying, motionless but whole, between the hounds.

"How do we lift him into it?" I pondered aloud, looking from him to the cart bed, some feet off the ground.

"Help me stand him as upright as possible and we'll bend him over the back. From there, we should be able to climb up and pull him in."

Thorn's dead weight was not as cooperative as Eudora's plan had erroneously predicted it would be. We were able to get him into a sitting position but struggled to lift him past that, neither of us having the required strength.

"We need to cut the ropes," I said. "We can put his arms around our shoulders and prop him up that way."

Eudora agreed. "It will be quicker to get a knife than fight with the knot."

I disappeared back into the house, running for the kitchen and its biggest blade. Before returning to Eudora, I checked quickly on Mr. Bentley, still in the billiard room, pale and sweating from pain.

"Tillie knows I was coming here," he said, teeth grinding even as he spoke. "Since I've not been home, she will come check eventually. Leave a note on the door for her in case you're not here when she does."

"We can stop along the way and tell her," I offered, sick at the thought of abandoning him, but his head twitched with a shake.

"Do not waste time. Go!"

I laid a kiss upon his cheek and rushed from the room for pen and paper. After hastily scribbling a note, I closed it in the front door in such a way that Mrs. Bentley's name, written in large letters across the top, was obvious, and brought the knife to Eudora.

"Mr. Bentley insists we leave him," I said as she sawed through the rope, half hoping she might have a better solution.

"We don't have much choice in the matter, but if all goes well, we'll be back by lunch."

"And if not?"

111

Instead of answering, Eudora pointed to the rope. "Here, hold this taut, it will help."

Once we'd freed Thorn, we were able to get ourselves under his arms and, on the count of three, leverage him almost to his feet. We staggered to the edge of the cart and draped his top half over the back while the dogs observed with tilted heads. Eudora climbed in and held Thorn in place.

"Come up and grab his other arm. Try to lift him enough his face doesn't drag against the wood."

With shaking limbs and perspiration sticking our clothes to us, we tugged Thorn little by little into the back of the cart, until only his feet hung over the edge. Eudora sat heavily on the side, fanning herself with her hand.

"My bag," she said while catching her breath. "I need it."

Though winded myself, I clamoured down and retrieved her satchel. It was heavier even than it looked and something within clinked as I handed it up to her.

"What is all that?"

"Protective measures mostly." She rifled through until she found what she was looking for, and pulled forth a bundled handkerchief tied off with a long, looped thread. She bent to pull it over Thorn's head and tucked it as best she could in his shirt. "Herbs to ward against harmful spirits. It should prevent possession.

"When we get to the cemetery, we will set up a circle bordered with salt, cold iron, and angelica incense. That, combined with the neutral ground, should prevent too thick a concentration of energy and will allow Thorn to safely confront his ghosts."

"What will he need to do?" I asked, studying my cousin's face from over the side of the cart. Even unconscious, there was a pull to his brow, as if peace still eluded him.

"He must acknowledge that he is the one holding on and give voice to his sorrow. Only once he releases it from himself will they also be freed." Eudora climbed over to the seat and took up the reins. "Pray, save the rest of your questions for the road and let us be on our way."

Instead of traversing through the village proper, a straighter path to the cemetery, we opted to go around to avoid slowing with the unwanted attention both Thorn and Eudora, dressed as she was, would have garnered. Cerberus and Black Shuck trotted alongside the cart, enjoying it as they would a normal morning stroll, and I sat, half-turned, on the bench to keep an eye on Thorn.

"The spirit who is attempting to possess him," I said, breaking the tense silence that had formed, bubble-like, around us, "how is such a thing possible?"

"Some dead are not content to remain so and seek hosts to feel the light of life again. They prey particularly on the downtrodden, easiest to manipulate and divide from others. Those made to feel most alone resist the least."

"That must be why he said I was meddling."

She made a noncommittal gesture.

I twisted my wedding ring around my finger, each answer only leading to new, terrible curiosity. "What happens to the host when the spirit is in their body?"

"I don't know. Accounts are sparse and undetailed. Apparently it's not something those who experience it are willing to discuss."

"Forgive yet another question," I said, hesitant to ask the next lest she take offence, "but how did you come to know all this? Was your great-aunt truly a witch as they say?"

"Necessity, and no, not as they say," she replied simply. "But that is not a story for now."

A deep bark from Black Shuck startled me, cutting off any additional queries to better understand Eudora, and I looked to the dog, focused on the road ahead with ears pricked forward. Cerberus came to run alongside him, so close their shoulders brushed, and he too let loose a softer trill. Following their gazes, I yelped.

"Eudora!"

"I see her."

A little girl stood alongside the lane, threadbare grey cape hugged around her small body. She lifted her face to the sound of the oncoming horse.

"She's one of the ghosts!"

Which meant Thorn was waking. I spun to find him beginning to fidget, still caught just on the other side of awareness.

Having reached the same conclusion, Eudora cursed and slapped the reins hard upon the horse's back. It kicked up its feet with a whinny and the cart creaked dangerously as it picked up speed. We careened past the child, and Eudora had to shout for her dogs when they fell behind with wagging tails at the waif's side. They whined, but a second call of their names was enough to have them bounding after us once more.

A smouldering figure shambled from the treeline, arms stretched in front of it, its hissing cry like a crow's caw. I had to cling to the cart to keep from being thrown as Eudora guided us around the burned ghost and urged the horse on even faster. The dogs bayed as they darted by it, but did not stop again.

Thorn groaned. "Netta? Oh, my head…"

"Stay still," I shouted, worried he might try to stand in his confusion.

"Where are we?"

"The gates are in sight! We won't be able to prepare properly, but we can make do. Get the salt and horseshoes from my bag," Eudora ordered, hunched so far forward with anticipation she was nearly off the seat.

"Who's that?" Thorn wondered groggily at the sound of Eudora's voice.

I almost didn't notice the broken boy stretched across the lane in front of us, so sudden was his appearance. We had no time to divert course and I screamed as we rolled over him, but there was no telltale bump or the sound of a human body trapped beneath our wheels. I wrenched around to see a waning mist where the boy had been. Cerberus and Black Shuck ran through it, dispersing it further so no trace of him remained.

"Netta," Thorn's hands grasped the back of the seat as he pulled himself forward. "What is going on?"

"The horseshoes and salt!" Eudora repeated sharply.

"Who *is* this?"

The horse shrieked and slowed suddenly, attempting a too-sharp turn that sent the cart skidding sideways as I reached for the satchel. I pitched forward, almost going headlong over the front. Only Thorn's fingers closing on my upper arm and yanking me back kept me in my seat. Though Eudora managed to get it under enough control to stop, the horse remained on the verge of flight, pawing the ground and snorting, its tail swishing. Breathing hard from my near tragedy, I looked up to see the cause of the poor animal's distress.

The drowned woman floated before the cemetery entrance, rotting arms snaking skyward.

Having noticed her too, Thorn fell back in the cart bed, head shaking, face drained of colour.

"We have to get into the cemetery quickly," Eudora said, hopping down between her waiting dogs.

"What's going on, Henrietta?" Thorn rasped. "Why are we here?"

"For you," I told him, crawling from the seat to kneel beside him. I took his face in my hands and made him look away from the writhing spirit, to me. "I need you to listen to me, Thorn. Eudora is here to help, but you must do as she says."

"What are you talking about?" he muttered, chest rising and falling rapidly. "Take me home at once."

"Please, cousin. I've seen the spirits; we all have. Don't deny it any longer! We know they are yours, that they haunt you. We only wish to help."

He pushed me away and lurched to his feet. "No. Whatever you think you're doing, stop. I told you not to concern yourself with this!"

A chill breeze swirled around us and the hounds emitted low growls, their hackles rising. Eudora snatched her bag from the cart. "We must hurry!"

I shuffled on my knees after Thorn, hands clasped in near prayer. "Thorn–"

"I do not need some stranger interfering in my business! I've told you, I'm fine. I can handle this on my own."

"That woman, she's gone," Eudora said, posture leery as she looked around. "We should take this opportunity to move into the cemetery before they manifest again."

"Thorn," I said again, so soft I barely heard myself, and reached out to take his wrist with tears burning down my cheeks. "It's alright. You do not need to carry this burden alone. I am here. I have *always* been here."

He swallowed hard, watery eyes fixed over my head. "You must think me so weak."

"Never!"

The exclamation was still on my lips when I was ripped backwards and flung out of the cart.

Chapter Fifteen

My shoulder took the brunt of my fall as I hit the ground and rolled to a dazed stop, the world little more than a smear of dark colour while I found my bearings. I groped along the ground to push myself up, but there was no grass or dirt beneath my hands. Only cold, hard cobblestone. I flung myself up in time with my heart leaping into my throat.

Grey surrounded me.

Grey city warehouses along a grey dock bordering a grey sea. I turned in place, my scuffling unbearably loud in the foggy silence. There was no lapping of water upon the wharf, no squalls from ever-hungry gulls, no life at all. Just my boot heels upon stone, and the relentless thump of my heart.

"Thorn?" I could not raise my voice above a whisper. "Eudora?"

I first went one way, hesitated, then turned toward the other, but neither direction seemed to lead anywhere better than the other and indecision held me.

Until the footsteps.

Heavy, calculating. They reverberated from all around, making it impossible to know where they were truly coming from. I made the choice from fear alone, racing down the port street while those steps fell once and again.

"*One lesson weren't enough, it seems,*" a man's gutteral growl pursued me as a blast of frigid wind. "*Let's teach you another then. Be a good girl and come here!*"

I buried my teeth in my knuckles to stop the building scream and turned down an alley between warehouses. It took me to another intersection, where I again chose without consideration, only seeking to put distance between myself and that voice. Each turn only led to more of the same towering facilities and narrow paths, all lacking any distinct markers that I might use to tell if I were going in circles. Still, I ran, every instinct telling me if I stopped, he would find me.

"*Come out, tart,*" he taunted from everywhere. "*Take your lesson!*"

The smack of heavy wood, a club or truncheon, echoed in the grey.

My nerves failed me and I dove behind a cluster of barrels, knees hugged to my chest and prayers falling from my lips. Movement fluttered in the corner of my eye and my breath hitched. Fog outlined a large shape standing at the end of the alley in front of me.

Its bark rumbled down the distance between us.

"Black Shuck?" I mouthed in disbelief.

He tossed his head and trotted off to the right.

I almost stayed put, convinced it had to be a trick or a desperate phantom of my own making, but when the wood smacked again, closer, I yelped and took off after the dog. Immediately a resounding footfall followed. With a strangled cry, I again saw a hound disappearing around a corner ahead and scrambled for him, both their names breaking from my lips.

"Black Shuck! Cerberus!"

I chased his shadow, aware of the beast looming at my back, each step bringing him closer.

"...following them..."

Eudora's voice cut faint as a dream through the city and I screamed for her, but she did not reply, nor did my cousin when I begged him to find me.

The first blow upon my back stole the air from me. The second sent me to my knees. I staggered forward, nails digging into stone until they broke as I tried to drag myself away. A foot caught me in the ribs, shoving me to my side. I curled into a sputtering ball, and through the spots filling my vision, a man stepped into view.

"...face them..." Eudora haunted me as I stared up, horror threatening to suffocate me.

His was a giant's height, standing head and shoulders even over Thorn. Shards of glass pockmarked corpse-white flesh, none more prominent than the jagged piece buried deep into his neck, and each thick limb jutted out at unnatural angles, dangling with a marionette's looseness. His movement was stilted, bowed legs twisting into each lumbering step, and the club he carried dragged behind him.

Red spattered lips curled into a vicious sneer I recognized right away. The same Thorn had worn when his body attacked me.

"*Bloody tarts.*" He hoisted the club, its bulky end level with my head. "*Always nosing around.*"

"...save her..."

I did what little I could to shield myself, weakly crying for my cousin, for my Victor, as it began to descend, and in the midst of my whispers, a roar.

"No!"

The man was set off balance midswing by its force and reared back, cracked teeth bared as the edges of the grey began to give way, like paint dripping down a canvas.

"I can't sleep."

My cousin's voice lifted in a snarl that melted away the nearest warehouse, revealing a series of headstones and angelic monuments. A strip of graveyard, with Thorn standing in a circle of Eudora's protections. She was behind him, a bowl of burning herbs cupped in her hands. Its smoke further pushed back the edges of ghostly influence. The dogs must have led me into the cemetery!

"I can't eat. Always I see them." Thorn crouched and came up with a pair of horseshoes. "And you."

The man bellowed, rage further misshaping his features, pinprick eyes burning into Thorn's, and he slammed his club into the ground. It did not crack against stone but thudded into soft earth.

Leaving the safety of the circle, Thorn stalked forward, and for the first time, uncertainty flickered in the ghostly visage as his cityscape receded before him.

War raged across my cousin's features in flashes of anger, sorrow, and anguish. "Ada was nine years old, so small for her age, and they left her in the cold. Her own parents! I carried her from the snowbank, the same way I carry my own daughter, and when I look into my arms, I see both their faces. How could they have put her out in that blizzard? How could no one else have noticed her? Why did no one save her?"

He swung one of the horseshoes, driving the glass-flecked ghost back a step.

"I named Matilda. She had no identity otherwise. No one came forth to claim the woman who washed ashore. She lay upon the coroner's slab, showing such marks of abuse beyond what the sealife had done. That was someone's child, wife, sister, something to someone! And yet she had no one at the end. Cruelty upon cruelty, and then to be denied even a name? I couldn't allow it."

He swung again, forcing aside the ghost's club, which disintegrated at the touch of cold iron.

"A grandfather burned in a house fire to collect an inheritance, a boy beaten and left for dead over the coins in his pockets. They were defenceless. Helpless! And in the course of my investigation, I was the villain, blamed for not doing enough sooner. For not saving them. How could I? What could I have done? I only needed someone to tell me and I would have done it!"

Smoke began to gather at the ghost's feet in attempt to escape, but Thorn rounded on him again with a horseshoe, this time connecting it with his face. The spectre howled with the burn of it.

"They were innocent! But not you, Philip Tenby. Your death was not my fault, and I refuse to hold it any longer."

"*You killed me, boy,*" the spirit, Philip, hissed in a vicious whisper, words worn so smooth this could not have been their first utterance. "*If you hadn't given chase, I'd not have gone through the window. You know I speak the truth!*"

"I have been prisoner to this guilt long enough," Thorn shouted, tears rolling freely down his face. "You will take no more of my life from me. Your actions led to your downfall, not mine! You murdered those women. You ran when caught. Those were your choices and your mistakes! But your worst one yet was trying to harm my sister."

His chest swelled with thunder and a storm burst from his throat as he brought the horseshoes down on either side of Philip Tenby's head. The iron cracked together, and the lasso of guilt that had held him to Thorn was undone.

The ghost bested, Thorn let the horseshoes slip from his hands and sank to his knees, body wracked with raw, open sobs. The fear and awe that had held me in its fist relinquished its hold, and I scrambled as quickly as I could through headstones to wrap my arms around him.

And for what felt like the first time in a long while, his found me too.

"I'm sorry," he said into my shoulder. "You deserve a better brother, one who is not so broken."

I forced him back so that our eyes met and shook my head. "Whatever state you are in, broken, drunk, haunted, there is no better brother I could ask for. And, whatever state you are in, I will be here to face it with you, always."

121

Epilogue

Holding one another up, we walked out of the cemetery with Eudora and her hounds. As Thorn helped me into the cart, four glimmers flickered in my periphery, and his was a sad smile that met my questioning look.

We arrived back to Daunderhead to find Mr. Bentley in the care of his wife, who had made the journey there shortly after our departure and were immediately taken under her wing to treat our various ailments. Eudora excused herself early on, certain we were in good hands, leaving Thorn to fill in the gaps I'd acquired at the cemetery.

After falling from the cart, they could see that I had come under the domination of the ghost, made potent by Thorn's furore. I was unresponsive to their calls, blind to their pursuit. What I had seen as a dockside had been in actuality the road away from the cemetery, an attempt to misguide me from our destination, but Black Shuck and Cerberus had stayed close to me, aware that something was wrong, and the ghost could not block them completely. Eudora would later credit their purity, God's own gift, for their ability to reach me when she and Thorn could not. Upon realising I was able to see the dogs, Eudora used them to lead me back into the cemetery while telling Thorn what had to be done.

Over the following days, while Mr. Bentley recuperated in Daunderhead and his wife continued to tend to us with all the fussiness of a mother hen, Thorn confided in me parts of himself he had attempted to bury, and from which the ghosts rose.

Before that day, he'd never spoken the name Philip Tenby to anyone unassociated with the case. Not even to Birdie.

He'd been a killer Thorn linked to multiple murders. Their final encounter had ended in a chase through the warehouse district, where Tenby fell through a window to his death. Plagued by guilt and believing himself responsible, his had been the first of Thorn's ghosts.

After so many sleepless nights wherein Tenby's final face waited in the dark, whispers began to fill his waking hours, reminders of the supposed blood upon his hands. While his professional circle lauded him for justice served, he could not see it the same. Justice would have been going before a court, having his crimes read out, a proper sentence. Not a single missed step, which Thorn blamed himself for. He never set out to kill a man, regardless of what that man had done. Execution was no province of his. But no one around him seemed to share in his conflicted feelings, and so he hid them behind a facade of pride.

People do not question the proud man. They do not look down upon him. Not like they would one besieged by remorse.

Unknowingly, he had reaped a fertile ground, and Ada grew from it next.

They had only just found out Birdie was pregnant when Thorn was called to investigate the body of a young girl found half buried in snow. In her, he saw his own future children, the things that could happen to them, the callousness of the world he was bringing them into. His heart broke for the daughter unloved, and he could not put her out of his mind as her parents had, sending her into a storm so they did not have to share their sup with her.

People do not question the stoic man. They do not believe him weak or doubt his ability to perform his duties. Not like they would one besieged by sorrow.

Then came Henry Evans, a pensioner whose heirs thought he'd outlived his usefulness, Oliver Payne, sixteen years old, who'd bragged to the wrong crowd about his first real wages, a nameless woman found in the surf.

In life, they had borne the worst of humanity, and in death, were held, in my opinion, by the best of it. A heart so gentle it broke anew each day he awoke to their faces.

But a man is not meant to be gentle. A man is not meant to break.

And so he hid, from them, from the shame of falling short of society's standards, from himself. Working himself to exhaustion with his off jobs allowed him some degree of freedom, denying the ghosts the focus and energy needed to take shape, but then night would come, bringing with it the nightmares. The bottle became his crutch, then his cage.

Thorn will never again be the boy I grew up with. The laughter that once came so easily to him is harder placed in a world he knows too well, having traversed its foulest depths.

What has been witnessed cannot be unseen, and it remains with him even now.

Eudora says it is a process, one he must allow himself to work through in full before he will truly be able to free himself from his hauntings.

There are bad days, where the bottles reappear and I catch glimpses of golden hair and crystal lashes, but they are fewer and far between, held at bay by the joy he finds with his wife and daughter, who came back to him after trading long, private letters, and in his new career as a village constable, a far more peaceful existence than a coroner's officer.

Upon the return of my parents, Thorn once more earned his way into Daunderhead through many long conversations over many long nights, allowing them to gain some understanding of what happened to us. To him. It was made simpler with Mr. Bentley's assistance, and the evidence of supernatural activity burned into the billiard room floor.

Thorn's is a heart wounded, and for so long we all took part in denying its healing. The depravity he was made to endure in his career and the expectations placed upon him have left their marks. Whether the scars ever fully close remains to be seen, though his family has rallied as a whole around him. Particularly Father, who has become closer to Thorn, and who has grown into a gentler man himself with his son's example.

For my part, I rarely rouse the ghosts anymore, only on the days I miss Victor most. I have not yet moved past my mourning and sometimes feel it is an impossible prospect. There is, however, a small comfort in truly knowing there is something beyond death. Perhaps, eventually, I will find my way to my beloved again.

In the meantime, I have formed an odd sort of kinship with Eudora Fellowes. I am fascinated by her. Though I am still not allowed to enter her home, I have forced my company on her to the point she has grudgingly accepted I will not be going away at any point in the near future and meets with me for regular lunches. She is like no other woman I've had the opportunity to meet, living entirely for herself and what makes her happy. I feel there is much I can learn from her, not only of the dead but of life, too.

She's a curious case, and I mean to study her.

At home, I fill my days with simple pleasures and family, making sure I am always available to Thorn especially. He still has trouble articulating his deeper, emotionally driven thoughts, a habit not yet fully formed, but sometimes merely sitting together in silence quiets his soul.

He has had a lifetime to learn what it means to be a man, and it may take a lifetime more to learn what it means to be Thorn.

It will be a long journey, one that will be dark at points, perhaps even haunted, but one he can be certain he will never have to make alone.

Afterword

A bereaved widow flees to the bosom of family and home. But family has been tainted, home's safety corrupted. In this high Gothic tale of love and loss, Netta Ward must confront her adopted brother's dissipation under the shadow of her own wrenching grief. Thorn is "drowning himself" in alcohol to avoid drowning in grief—and it's Netta's love that illuminates the path through his pain, just as he brightens Netta's way through hers.

At its core, S.H. Cooper's *Bottling His Ghosts* is a crushing portrayal of grief. Netta finds herself "at violent odds with a world that I knew longer knew my place in" as she travels back to Daunderhead Hall, which remains cruelly unchanged in the midst of her grief: "I wanted to rage against Daunderhead and beat upon its stones for not crumbling with me." She yearns for her lost husband; she finds herself adrift without him.

Thorn's grief, vividly externalized as ghosts, has driven him to what Victorians frankly knew as dissipation. Drinking himself to insensibility silences the sorrow he soaked up as a coroner's officer. But Netta refuses to abandon her adopted brother to the bottle. Not only does she share in his grief, she helps him conquer it, and in doing so, begins to heal her own. Only through others, Cooper teaches us, are we healed.

The author brings this historic Victorian tale to life through tense plotting as she threads through classic Gothic motifs. Sprawling Daunderhead is the haunted, stately Gothic manse, ghost-stricken.

Netta, our plucky heroine, may be prone to fainting but persists through terrible odds. Eudora Fellowes, the gender-flouting, independent witch on the hill, stands outside of social norms to problematize and intrigue our heroine. The supernatural looms. The dead walk. But Cooper's vivid characterization twists these tropes and snatches them for her own. *Bottling His Ghosts* remains a singular tale of the ties that bind, the enduring and stubborn love of a sister for her adopted brother.

Again and again, *The Selected Papers from the Consortium for Anomalous Phenomenon* has returned to the family. In *Family Solstice*, Kate Maruyama examines family ties, sibling relationships, and generational sin; in *12 Hours*, L. Marie Wood's nameless narrator yearns to connect with his child and wife. Sarah Hans's *Asylum* deals with found family; David Sandner's *His Unburned Heart* sees Mary Shelley searching for her husband's heart. In *Hollow Tongue* and *Errant Roots*, both Eden Royce and Sonora Taylor, respectively, examine generational trauma as narrators return to their family of origin. Likewise, my own *Blood Cypress* finds Lila Carson coping with familial sin.

If one theme unites the novella series, it's family: how do we live with those we love? How do we cope with their transgressions, with the trauma they inflict? How do we deal with missed connections and lost opportunities? How do we count the ways they hurt us? In *Bottling His Ghosts*, Netta's love for Thorn conquers his darkness and leads him home. The positive ending is typical of historical Gothic novels, and it's the brightest conclusion of the series. Mary Shelley gets Percy's heart back, but she still must cope with the bitterness of his death. *Errant Roots'* Deirdre escapes her family, but she is not unscathed. And Hans's protagonist Ashleigh carries part of the asylum with her when she leaves. Other endings—well, the best description may be "complicated," at best (*Bleak Houses*), and "downright disastrous" at worst (our Southern Gothics, *Hollow Tongue* and *Blood Cypress*).

Family, concludes *The Selected Papers*, is a complicated, bloody beast. We yearn for connection. So often, we fail. We fall short. We falter, trembling at the cusp of understanding. We may suffer for the horrors done before us, perhaps stretch for those closest to us. But in the end, S.H. Cooper hands us this: Connection is possible. Hope is real. Death is not the end, and in one another, we find our way home.

About the Author

S.H. Cooper is a Florida based author of horror and fantasy. When not writing, she enjoys playing video games, watching horror films, and looking for any excuse not to leave her house so she can sing nonsensical songs to her husband and pets. You can find her online at www.authorshcooper.com or on most social media platforms as Pippinacious or S.H. Cooper.

www.ingramcontent.com/pod-product-compliance
Lightning Source LLC
Chambersburg PA
CBHW052011240626
47153CB00008B/2837